EVA

Boyd C. Hipp, II

Mahalo Books—Greer, SC
ISBN: Pending
Library of Congress Control Number: pending
Title: EVA
Author: Boyd C. Hipp, II
Digital distribution | 2021
Paperback | 2021

This is a work of fiction. The characters, names, incidents, places, and dialogue are products of the author's imagination, and are not to be construed as real.

Dedication

When I wrote Mahalo Memories, I not only acknowledged the two men who made the book possible but I included an acknowledgement to my children as well. Therefore, it seems only natural to dedicate this sequel to the next generation, my grandchildren. Here's to you Elizabeth, Sarah, Charlie, Caroline, Cate, Annie, Calhoun, Hodges, Thomas, Martha, and to all those who are to follow.

Thank you for making my life immeasurably better!

Tight lines and good fishing to you all. I love you.

Poppy
November, 2021

Other Novels by Boyd Hipp

Mahalo Memories

"Everyone has one book in them.
Almost nobody has two."

Bruce Butler
The Affair

Acknowledgements

When I write a book based upon part fiction and part actual events, it helps to have my own army of folks who were actually there and could add their own experiences.

My sincerest gratitude to the following who gave life to this story. In no particular order they are:

Captain Mac Finch, Gage Caulder, Mary Haddow, Neel Hipp, Major Jimmy Stewart (USAF Ret.), Shufy Rowe, Mary Jane Jacques and Jean Rowe.

And to Kim Mann for her insights and technical expertise.

Prologue

Bimini, Bahamas
Summer 1969

It was getting late and Calhoun, along with Bones and Hank, was getting nervous. Where was she? She should have been back by now. He had abandoned his boat, the Mahalo, due to its confined area, in favor of the dock where he paced back and forth. His strides were only interrupted by his furtive glances toward the end of the dock where it met land. His hopes that he might see her round the corner diminished with every moment.

"Gentlemen, we have to go. I cannot sit here any longer without knowing. Let's start heading toward the Anchors Aweigh. At the very least we can have a drink at the Compleat Angler." Calhoun's ever-present pipe was clinched tightly between his teeth as he spoke.

Captain Hank already had the keys to the salon doors on this 50-foot Hatteras Sport Fisher. "Let me lock up unless Bones you want to stay and wait on Eva?" The stare Bones gave Hank quickly answered that question. Hank took a moment to reach into one of the drawers in the tackle box where he pulled out a billy club. Normally used to knock out fish that were still aggressive once boated, he tossed it to Calhoun. "Boss, I hope we don't need this but I thought I would let you hang on to it in case we do."

"God, I hope it does not come to that," replied Calhoun as he set a fast pace down the dock which grew even faster as he got closer to the road. Hank and Bones trailed after him by just a couple of footsteps.

Chapter One

Trapped! Eva stood in the middle of the floor at the Compleat Angler, head down, shoulders stooped forward in a sign of utter defeat. How could she have been so stupid as to be led here? It was true, she thought. You really can see your life flash by when you think you may be at the end. Well, it really was no more than the last three plus years where her thoughts took her but it was that life she wanted to focus on anyway.

It was here she had left the thug, Slayder, who was now sitting at this empty bar with a Cheshire catlike grin etched across his face while holding a six-inch boning knife known for its sharp point and even sharper edges. Oh, how she would like to slap the grin right off of him! It was here she had caught her first glimpse of the man she had fallen in love with…Calhoun. It was here she had enjoyed so many fine evenings with Calhoun, his boat captain Hank and the affable native first mate, Bones.

She stared at the wooden plank floor, never having really paid it any attention over the last three years. Discarded peanut shells littered the area where Slayder now sat. The smell of stale beer and cigarette smoke permeated the room along with the faint whiff of another odor she recognized but could not place. If I'm going to die, she thought, it won't be on his terms.

"What do you want Slayder?" she yelled, pulling herself upright in an act of defiance. But before he could answer she spun around to face Slayder's apparent accomplice Bowers, who had been, until a few moments ago, Bones' trusted cousin.

"And you…you, you Judas! How dare you!" she yelled with such vehemence that Bowers flinched and took an involuntary step backwards before he could gather himself.

"Nothing personal" came the reply. "It was only business".

"Well, you son of a bitch, I hope you got your thirty pieces of silver!"

Before she could turn back toward Slayder, she was assailed once more by that familiar odor. What was it?

She shook her head as she turned back toward Slayder, as if she were trying to loosen up those cobwebs which may be blocking her memory.

Slayder stood, now facing this blond-haired beauty with her hands curled into fists. "Before you get too worked up Eva, I only arranged this meeting to remind you of the money your paramour owes me for the drugs you guys had me busted for. Cover my loses and we are done with each other."

Eva could not help but smile, which really looked more like a smirk given how agitated she was as she recalled the incident at Honeymoon Beach where the crew of the Mahalo had called in local law enforcement resulting in the confiscation of over one million dollars of marijuana and the jailing of Slayder and two of his henchmen. While Slayder ultimately escaped, his fellow cohorts were not so lucky and were both serving time in federal prison.

"He has the money and if any of your contacts were any good you would know that. He plans on… "PRINCE ALBERT! I SMELL PRINCE ALBERT!" she yelled triumphantly.

The look of confusion on Slayder's face barely had time to form when the entire bar exploded into the sound of mayhem.

Chapter Two

The door to the Compleat Angler was never meant to withstand a concentrated attack. Just as Eva was yelling, Bones had gotten a running start and with the force of an NFL linebacker, he lowered his shoulder and slammed into the obstacle standing between the crew of the Mahalo and Eva. The door gave way so quickly, splintering into a million shards of wood, that it caused Bones to lose his balance and go tumbling into the bar where he collided with Bowers, knocking them both to the floor.

"Don't let him go Bones, he is in cahoots with Slayder!" instructed Eva. "Calhoun, Slayder is right there." She yelled, pointing at a rapidly retreating figure who was headed toward a door located at the back of the bar. Calhoun took the billy club and flung it end over end, catching Slayder solidly in the back of the head.

"Oomph" was the guttural noise from Slayder as he staggered, placing his hand on his head where he had been hit, blood already gushing between his fingers. Despite his injury, he made it to and out the back door.

"Hank!" yelled Calhoun. "Get after Slayder. He's hurt so you should be able to catch him."

Without another word, Hank was running toward the rear door, out the back and down the docks toward the harbor. He caught sight of Slayder, staggering down the docks as if he had been on a weekend bender. Blood now soaked the back of his shirt where the billy club had struck as a result of the club cracking his head. Hank knew that scalp wounds bled profusely. He also knew an injured and cornered animal was extremely dangerous so he slowed his run to a fast gait, closing the distance between the two men.

"Slayder, give it up man. It's over." Hank called out. Slayder stopped and looked back at the approaching captain, giving a smile which Hank would later describe as pure evil. As he did so, he leaned over and fell between two boats into the cool night waters of the harbor and disappeared.

Chapter Three

"Slayder!" yelled Hank as he raced to the spot where their mutual nemesis had fallen? Jumped? Hank could not be certain which act he had just witnessed, he just knew Slayder was nowhere to be seen as the captain ran back and forth on the docks trying to glimpse the drug dealer swimming away or worse yet, a body floating out with the tide.

Nothing! The sound of multiple footfalls made him turn to see who was running down the dock.

"Well, well. A little late don't you think?" retorted Hank to U.S. Marshall Chewning and his men. "Where the hell were you guys? As a matter of fact, where was everyone on this damn island who was supposed to be watching over Eva?" Chewning had been working this case for several weeks now in an attempt to close this drug ring. It was his idea in fact to use Eva as bait to draw Slayder out. He knew Slayder was still enamored with her but he also knew his greed could possibly lead to an error in judgment allowing the Federal Agents to catch Slayder. Instead, it had almost gotten Eva killed.

"You sound just like your boss" Chewning answered. "He screamed the same exact thing when we came barging through the door. I take it Slayder has disappeared once again?"

"Either disappeared or is dead. He took a pretty good whack on the head from the billy club Calhoun threw at him. He was pretty woozy when he fell or jumped into the water."

"Well, there is nothing more we can do here until we can get a boat in the water to run a search."

"We have a seventeen-foot Mako tied up alongside the Mahalo, keys are in the cup holder and there is a hand-held spotlight underneath the console so why don't your two associates go make good use of it?"

All it took was a nod of the head from Agent Chewning and both men were off at a dead run toward the Big Game Club where the Mahalo was docked.

Hank immediately turned his attention to the federal agent standing before him. "You wanted to use Eva as bait to draw out this so-called drug gang promising to keep her under watch but when it came down to the rubber meeting the road, you and everyone else on this island had disappeared. What the hell is going on?"

The anger in Hank's voice coupled with his clenching and unclenching his fists made Agent Chewning realize he had better choose his next words and actions carefully.

"Honestly Captain, I don't how but I suspect some of those answers may be in there." as he nodded toward the bar. "Let's go find out".

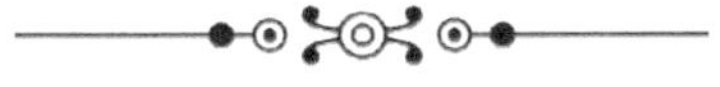

Chapter Four

The two men walked into a cacophony of shouts and cries. Bones had Bowers by the throat demanding answers to questions he could not have responded to even if he wanted as the reddish-purple color of his face underscored the obvious fact that Bones was moments away from killing the man. Agent Chewning quickly intervened by pulling Bones off the stricken culprit and placed himself between the two. "ENOUGH!" screamed the lawman. "This man is in my custody and will be sent stateside for further prosecution as well as apparently for his own protection." Bones immediately stopped and turned his attention to Eva who was sobbing in Calhoun's arms, shaking fiercely, as it appeared she may be going into shock.

"Are you okay, Eva?" Bones inquired with genuine concern.

"I'll be fine. I'm angrier than anything else. Where was everybody that was supposed to be watching over me while I came back from dinner? Hell, half the island followed me to dinner but the streets were empty when I left. Bowers was the only friendly face I saw and that turned out to be not so friendly."

"I can answer that" volunteered Bones. "Before I nearly killed my cousin, he did tell me he had relayed the message for everyone to go home, that we no longer needed anyone else to escort you to the Mahalo. That's why the streets were empty."

Agent Harris took the lead at this point. "What did Slayder want?"

Eva gave a shiver as she recalled the brief but intense meeting. "He still wants the money he lost in the drug bust over on Honeymoon Beach. In his irrational mind it is our fault he got busted. The only positive thing I heard him say was that we would be left alone once he got his losses covered. It was at that moment I realized what else I was smelling in this bar…Prince Albert pipe tobacco. I knew Calhoun was close by then so I yelled out to give you guys an idea as to where I was."

Calhoun took that moment to release the stem of his pipe from his tightly clenched teeth. "Hell, I didn't even realize I still had this pipe in my mouth!"

The confusion on his face along with his genuine puzzlement over still having the pipe in his mouth proved to be the ideal stress breaker as everyone got a laugh from his confession.

The moment was broken by the sound of an outboard motor approaching the docks. It was the other two agents looking for any sign of Slayder.

"Anything?" yelled Agent Chewning.

"Not yet. We are going to look up and down the marina and out into the harbor. If he is dead, his body could be anywhere. Pinned under a dock, wedged between two boats or fish food out in the middle of the harbor. We'll keep searching.

By the way, we bumped into a couple of policemen out on patrol and asked that they get some folks down here to aid in the search for Slayder so you should have some company soon."

About ten minutes later, four members of the Royal Bahamas Police Force appeared and began a more thorough search of the marina. It was determined the tide was coming in so they turned their efforts to under the docks and any place around the seawall where a body could get snagged.

Chewning approached Calhoun and Eva as they had not moved far from the table where they had initially sat.

"Look, this is going to be a long night. You guys have done more than your part. Get back to the boat and get some rest. For now, you both are guests of the Bahamas so don't plan on leaving until we say so. Got it?"

Calhoun and Eva nodded their heads in unison. They turned to Hank and Bones who were standing nearby and without a word spoken between them, they all got up and moved toward the door to leave.

"One more thing." yelled Chewning. "You contact us if Slayder shows up…right?"

"Not a problem, agent." responded Calhoun as the four hustled out of the Compleat Angler and headed toward the Big Game Club and the Mahalo which awaited their arrival.

Chapter Five

They took their time heading back to the Mahalo. Eva was tucked protectively under Calhoun's arm while Hank and Bones flanked the couple, one on each side. Eva kept her head down which caused her to really notice for the first time the composition of the hard packed dirt road. Aside from the harden dirt itself, interspersed were large smooth rounded stones. No doubt this was representative of some long-ago sailing ships ballast, trading the weight of these stones for barrels of rum that was produced in the area. Funny how you see things for the first time when a little trauma has occurred in your life, Eva thought.

When they got to the docks of the Big Game Club, Bones gave Hank a quizzical look.

"No need for you to follow us to the boat, Bones. It's late and we have it from here. Why don't you come by mid-morning tomorrow and if we are not under total lock and key perhaps we can run to Lion's Beach and do a little light tackle fishing along the way."

"Sounds good Cap. Eva, you get some rest. I'm sorry we put you through all of this."

His concern was met with a weak but silent smile. Calhoun nodded his thanks to his first mate as he joined Hank and Eva heading toward the boat to get the rest they all craved. Even though it was barely past midnight, they all felt the strain of a very long day.

Chapter Six

When they arrived at the boat, Hank insisted on going through it first to make sure no one was lurking inside. It took less than a minute to clear the Mahalo and just another minute before the sound of the shower could be heard coming from the master stateroom.

Hank and Calhoun gathered in the main salon as they both needed a drink while Eva showered. Calhoun took three fingers of scotch while Hank doubled up on his rum for his rum and Coke, barely introducing the Coke to his glass. They both sat in silence for a few moments before Calhoun broke the quiet.

"Tough day on us all. I hope we can bring Eva around. She seems more introspective but I guess that is to be expected."

"I believe if we can get back on the water and change the scenery a bit, it can only serve to lift her spirits. She is too energetic to let this affect her for long. She'll be fine. Perhaps a day over at

Lions Beach tomorrow will be the tonic the captain ordered!" Hank observed.

They both heard the shower cut off at the same time followed by an urgent but firm command, "Calhoun, can you come down here?"

"Looks like my night may not be quite over" he said with a wink towards his captain. "See you in the morning." Hank was left in the salon to contemplate the occurrences of the entire day.

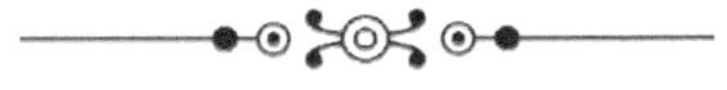

Chapter Seven

Eva patted the bed beside her as Calhoun came into the stateroom.

"Come hold me Calhoun. I need the feel of decent humanity next to me."

He quickly put his unfinished drink on the nightstand and disrobed to his boxers. No words were spoken as Eva held him tight. She started kissing him, slowly at first then ravenously as she reclaimed her place in the human race. Their lovemaking was brief but intense as afterwards they both fell immediately into a deep sleep.

"Uhh? What?" It was Eva. She had awakened to a noise she could not place. She glanced at the luminous dial on her watch. Four a.m. She patted the bed expecting to find a slumbering Calhoun only to find the space next to her warm but empty which caused her to sit bolt upright. She saw him standing at the door looking back at her signaling to be quiet with his index finger pressed across his lips.

He opened the door to the hallway to see Hank going by, a machete in hand. "I didn't know you had a machete captain" he whispered as he joined Hank in the hallway. It seemed an inane statement at the time but it was the only thing that immediately came to mind.

"I take it you heard it too" responded the captain.

"Yeah, footsteps on the deck above our stateroom. Someone is on the Mahalo."

"Let's go find out who our visitor is" suggested Hank.

They opened the salon doors and stepped outside to the cockpit which was most often the scene of battles with the fish they boated. Tonight, they were met with a shroud of fog, obscuring anything beyond three feet. Their tension was almost palpable so it did not help when Eva slinked up behind them causing both men to jump when she asked what was going on.

"Someone is walking on the bow." Hank responded. "Calhoun, you and Eva go around the starboard side, closest to the dock, I'll go around on the other side and will meet you forward at the anchor locker."

Since it seemed to Calhoun the less talking the better, he simply grabbed Eva's hand and the two of them started edging along the side of the boat toward the bow. The mist hung so deeply it blanketed everything in dampness making footing even more precarious than it normally was as they edged along the catwalk. It occurred to Calhoun he would probably bump into whoever was on the boat before he could see him given how thick the fog was but there was nothing he could do about the weather.

Seconds later they both emerged onto the bow and headed toward the anchor locker located on the port side where Hank had just arrived.

"Nothing," reported the captain, "except this" as he pointed to the deck.

There, on the wet deck were a clearly visible set of footprints. They seemingly materialized out of nowhere and trailed across the entire bow, from port to starboard and disappeared as they would have come to the dock.

"Oh, swell" Eva shivered as she spoke. "Now we have ghosts just appearing from nowhere?"

"I doubt there is anything otherworldly about these" Calhoun observed. "Someone was here for whatever reason but they are gone now. No need trying to find them in this fog. Best we can do is look around in the morning and let Agent Chewning know what happened here tonight."

"Well, I for one will not be able to get back to sleep so what about a really early breakfast guys?" chirped a newly revitalized Eva.

"Besides, I have a new project I want to tackle later this morning and Hank's machete is just the tool I need."

"Calhoun and Hank gave each other quizzical stares as Hank whispered, "She's back!"

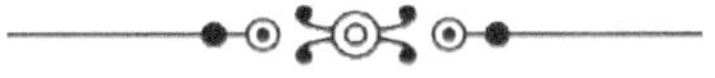

Chapter Eight

"There is nothing better than French Toast made with Bimini Bread!" proclaimed Eva. Judging from the satiated smiles she received in return there would be no argument from either Hank or Calhoun. The sun was beginning to make its appearance, burning off the fog in the process, and it was evident Eva was ready to get on with her day.

"Now, who is going to go find Marshall Chewning to let him know what happened here last night? I think we should do it now before the docks fill up with people and destroy any evidence out there if there is any." Eva had taken charge so the two men waited their instructions.

"I'll go" volunteered Hank. "I want to walk down the dock anyway to see if I can find anything."

"Perfect. Calhoun, you and I are going to move into the Big Game Club tonight. I don't know how long we are going to be kept here while the investigation runs its course, but I do not want to stay on this boat while party's unknown are creeping around on it."

"Understood." came the reply while he loaded his pipe bowl with fresh tobacco from his can of Prince Albert. He fired up his bowl and leaned back in his chair to observe Eva as she plotted out their day.

"Lord, she is too cute for her own good," he thought. When she was animated like this the smattering of freckles across the bridge of her nose seemed to highlight the twin dimples which appeared every time she smiled which was a lot right now. It literally tugged at his heart and he felt like some schoolboy with his first teenage crush. And perhaps he was, only difference was this crush had been going on better than three years and he was far from a teenager. He shook his head as he realized this was a whole lot more than just a crush but how glorious it was to still feel this way. God, how he loved this woman!

"CALHOUN! Are you listening to me?"

"Sorry, I was daydreaming." came the meek reply.

"I was asking if we had any spare soup bowls on board. Have you noticed the number of stray dogs on this island? They're everywhere, especially on the docks when the boats come in from a day of fishing."

"No, we don't have any spare bowls, only the cereal bowls we use every day. Eva, try as you might, you can't save the world, no matter how noble the cause."

"I may not save the world but I can damn sure save a few dogs! Now, where is Hank's machete?"

Chapter Nine

Calhoun found himself at the base of a coconut palm tree, watching as Eva scampered up the spine of the tree heading toward the area where coconuts hung. With a machete tucked into her beltloops, she looked like some sort of modern-day pirate ready to board an opposing ship. All Calhoun needed was an ARRG! MATEY! and the scene would be complete.

"Please be careful," he yelled as Eva climbed higher, her bare feet slipping ever so slightly on the still damp trunk.

A fine sheen of sweat had broken out over her forehead and neck, coating her back and arms in perspiration making it ever more difficult to hang on. Her concentration was entirely focused on getting to the three or four coconuts now within her range. She sat down, straddling the tree and removed the machete from her belt. With a wild swing, the momentum which nearly took her down, she managed to knock two of the coconuts down where they fell inches from Calhoun.

"That's enough" he yelled up to her. "Let's not overachieve on your first day!"

Eva sat there for a moment deciding whether to continue on her coconut crusade but decided she had enough to see if her idea would work. "Look out below" she shouted as she dropped the machete which ended up sticking straight into the mushy ground like some version of giant mumbley-peg. She then slid down the back of the tree, landing gracefully on both feet and secretly happy she had not caught a splinter in a place where splinters did not belong.

Calhoun started clapping, applauding her athletic prowess.

"Now what?" he queried.

Her impish smile returned, revealing once again her deep-set dimples and firing up her green eyes. "Gather up those two coconuts and follow me back to the Mahalo" came the command. A brief glance at her watch revealed it was only seven a.m. "Look at everything we have accomplished and its barely seven!"

"And it may be best if you spend the balance of this day somewhere else!" She turned to the voice she recognized to see Agent Chewning standing there with a whole cadre of Bahamian Police.

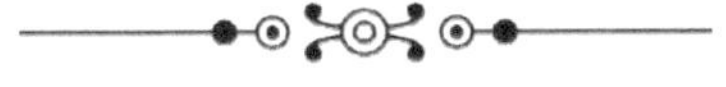

Chapter Ten

"We have not found a body or even a part of a body so far." They were back on the Mahalo as Agent Chewing was giving them an update while the police scoured the area around the Big Game Club in hopes of turning up some clue as to who had been deck dancing last night on the Mahalo.

The entire Mahalo crew was present Hank, Eva, Calhoun and Bones who had also been unable to sleep and was headed to the boat until he bumped into the parade of police headed in the same direction.

"So, are we able to move about today as long as we do not leave Bahamian jurisdiction?" inquired Calhoun.

"You may go fishing, or whatever you wish as long as you check in by radio every hour and I want you back at this dock by five so we can lock you down for the night. Deal?"

"Deal!" They all said in unison and even rose together to get ready to get underway as they showed Chewning the door. "We'll see you tonight" Eva volunteered and with that Hank took to the bridge to start the engines while Bones made his way to the fish locker to start preparing baits.

The Mahalo was coming alive as she was readied to do what she was built to do …. fish! Coconuts could wait.

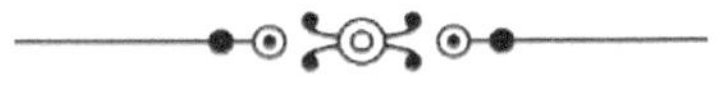

Chapter Eleven

There was a new attitude aboard the Mahalo. The previous evenings encounters put into a rear-view mirror. As they cleared the jetties, Hank headed due north and east with the destination being Lions Beach. Bones put out some of the lighter tackle, not expecting anything too big since they would be running in relatively shallow waters.

Hank almost immediately spotted a weed line and where those lines were usually lurked dolphin. He yelled down to Bones, pointed out what he saw and told him to put two lines in the water. Calhoun and Eva assumed their positions in their respective fighting chairs. A sense of normalcy settled in.

ZIP ZING! "Two!" yelled Hank as Calhoun's rod bent over. Calhoun managed to get the rod out of its side holder and into the middle cup and start reeling. Hank throttled back to reduce speed. Bones stood guardian between the two chairs, willing to lend assistance if necessary. Then, there it was again, ZIP ZING as Eva's line popped out of the outrigger and her rod took on a similar bend.

She leaned over and tried to get her rod out of its holder but the angle and weight were too much so Bones grabbed it and put the rod into the holder between her legs.

While this was going on, Hank slipped quietly past both anglers and into the salon to grab a bag of garbage he had earlier placed in a white plastic bag. Allowing Bones to shield him from the anglers he returned to the bridge, garbage in hand and slung the bag as far as he could on the opposite side of the boat away from Eva who never heard the splash given her distraction.

"Dolphin. I think mine is about ready to boat" announced Calhoun. "Seems small but I know that can be the best to eat." Just then the bag of garbage went floating by. The sight of the garbage never failed to get Eva upset as to how people could pollute the ocean. The truth was, in the absence of any other landmark, Hank used the bag as a marker letting him know the location where he had gotten the strike so he could circle back to that spot. After all the fishing they had done, Eva never caught on that Hank was the culprit although she strongly suspected he was involved.

Bones got Calhoun's line rebaited and into the water just as Eva's line came up. In fact, Bones did not have time to get Calhoun's line in the rigger as it was hit as Bones was spooling line out. This prompted Hank to come down and give a hand as both anglers were now into the fish.

"Barracuda" announced Bones regarding what Calhoun had. This fish was about fifteen pounds and gave a bit more of a fight. Hank took a nice twelve-pound dolphin off Eva's line, rebaited it and got it into the outrigger when it was hit again. Another dolphin.

"Now this is fun!" yelled Eva in triumph as she began reeling in another dolphin. Hank made the turn back toward the garbage bag where they hooked up with two more dolphin. It was in the next turn where something happened which Hank had experienced many times in the past... the activity stopped. After Eva got her fish boated, there were no more strikes. It was strange how every fish had disappeared. Hank took time during the lull to check in with Agent Chewning. After a quick update as to their position and destination, Chewning responded there had been no sighting of Slayder. He had vanished once again. This was news Hank decided to keep to himself until later.

Chapter Twelve

They made the approach to Lions Beach at almost idle speed. The turquoise waters lapped gently onto the undisturbed white sandy beach, capped by a large white house perched on a bluff above.

"Why have we never been here Hank?" asked Eva as she marveled at the scene in front of her. "We always seem to go to Honeymoon Beach but this is even prettier and more isolated." The last statement brought a gleam to her eye that only Calhoun caught, causing him to smile.

"You are about to find out" responded the captain as he pulled the throttles back to neutral causing the Mahalo to gently beach herself. As soon as she did, Eva got her answer. Like Honeymoon Beach where they were besieged by flies the moment they brought out food, these flies did not wait. And worse yet they were huge, vicious and obviously hungry horseflies. Their bites were painful and plentiful. Immediately Hank put the boat in reverse and pulled back about fifty yards from the beach where the flies did not bother them.

"Who could live here with those things?" exclaimed Eva. "No wonder the beach is empty. Who owns that house on the bluff and why would they build here?" Her questions flew out in a torrent and only Hank's rebuff stopped them.

"Easy, there Eva. I don't know who owns that house. As long as I have been here that house has been there. I've never seen anyone around it but someone maintains it because it is always in great shape and seems to always be freshly painted. I tried one time to run up the bluff to check it out but the horseflies drove me back before I could make it halfway up. We're safe here. For whatever reason they won't come this far out. Same thing we witnessed when we had lunch at Honeymoon Beach. Anyway, as long as we're here, take a look down at the bottom."

Given that the waters were crystal clear and only slightly opaque, it was evident there were multiple brown smudges scattered across the area.

"What are those?" asked the ever-inquisitive Eva.

"Conch. Now why don't you make yourself useful and dive for a few. It's about fifty feet to the bottom so you can make that. Bring me up about a dozen or so and I will make a conch salad while we are here."

Needing no further encouragement, Eva grabbed a mesh dive bag along with a mask and snorkel and got to work.

It took her five trips to gather a dozen conch primarily due to the size and the weight of the conch which filled the bag quickly. She was exhausted when she was done but not so much so that she couldn't stand and watch as Hank took a ballpein hammer to chisel out the top of the conch shell exposing the meat inside. He reached in and grabbed the conch and placed it on a platter liberally covering it in freshly squeezed lime juice which served to 'cook it'. He made a salad of chopped onion, green peppers and tomatoes along with his secret sauce over a bed of lettuce. He would chop the conch later after it had time to marinate.

"Now let's put this in the refrigerator for a while to cool down. Eva, if you and Calhoun want to swim for a minute, now's the time."

Calhoun needed no further encouragement as he was diving into the cool Bahamian waters practically before Hank had finished talking. Since they could not swim to shore without being attacked, they settled for just swimming around the Mahalo. Calhoun swam by the anchor which was firmly dug into the sandy bottom just to make sure it was holding. While he was there, he spied a starfish so he dove on it gathering it up for Eva.

Treading water, he showed her his catch. "See all those feet on the bottom of this starfish? That's how they walk on the bottom."

Intrigued, Eva took the starfish from him saying "I want to see more," as she swam back toward the dive platform holding the starfish high above her head.

The four of them were gathered around the dining table as the Mahalo gently rocked at anchor.

"This salad is fabulous Hank!" proclaimed Eva. "Although it is a bit chewy, like munching on a bunch of rubber bands. But the flavor is beyond description."

"No offense taken." replied the captain turned chef. "I did not have the time to use the mallet on it to tenderize the meat nor did we have the time to let it marinate as long as I would like. All in all, it came out pretty well as I see no one has anything left on their plate. In the meantime, have you observed your starfish friend?"

When Calhoun and Eva had returned from their swim, Eva had challenged Hank as to how starfish moved. She was convinced they swam while both Hank and Calhoun insisted, they walk on the hundreds of feelers underneath them. To prove the point, Hank had placed the starfish in the middle of the fishbox before lunch. As Eva looked out the salon doors, she could see the starfish had almost walked off the far edge.

"Okay, you win. But at least now I can say I've been conching."

"Conching?" chimed in a puzzled Bones.

"Sure, isn't that what I did? Gathering up the conch for lunch."

"Well, I've never heard it called that but I guess that is what it could be called."

"See, Eva, you have created a new term. I'll be sure to look for it in the next Webster's." teased Calhoun as he stood up to start washing dishes.

"Folks, since it is going on midafternoon, I suggest we head back so Agent Chewning doesn't get worried."

"Okay by me captain" Eva responded. "Besides, I have a chore to perform with those

coconuts I got this morning that you three hunks
can help me with."

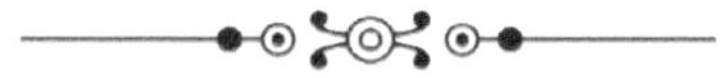

Chapter Thirteen

It was going on four P.M. when the Mahalo pulled back into their berth at the Big Game Club. As was the routine, Bones threw the spring lines to whomever may be on the dock to assist. This time it happened to be Agent Chewning. Once the bow and stern lines were also secure, Hank cut off the engines.

"Permission to come aboard?" queried Chewning.

"Do we have a choice?" spat back Eva who was still furious about being led in as a sacrificial lamb the previous evening in a futile attempt to corral the drug smuggling Slayder.

"I won't be a minute." replied Chewning as he took a step down into the cockpit. "I just want to give you a quick update, which there is no update. We have not recovered a body so we have to assume Slayder is still alive and is somewhere still on the island. We will keep an extra man here tonight to make sure you folks stay safe."

"Boy, don't I feel safe now!" retorted Eva over her shoulder as she slid open the salon doors and disappeared inside.

Chewning was clearly exasperated by the entire situation as it was obvious that Slayder continued to seemingly stay one step ahead of the police. "Sorry if she offends you Agent Chewning but she does have a point." offered up Calhoun. "Thanks for the extra security but the best thing you can do for us is to allow us to go home."

"I agree!" chimed in Eva as she reappeared from the salon with machete in hand. "Now if you don't mind, we have some work to do."

Without any further acknowledgement of the exasperated agent, Eva stepped around him and stepped onto the dock.

"Calhoun, toss me the coconuts and come help me with splitting them open."

As Bones began to wash down the Mahalo from the day's sea spray, Calhoun carried the coconuts up onto the dock and followed Eva to the grassy area outside the Big Game Club. She instructed him to cut them in half which took a few good whacks with the machete but finally got the job done. She then produced a carving knife she had brought along and carved out the coconut meat leaving a hollow bowl as a result.

"Viola!" she trumpeted triumphantly. "Now we have bowls for these stray dogs we see everywhere. My hope is people will use these to help feed them." She turned to Calhoun with her green eyes blazing with delight. "What do you think?"

"I think you are genius, beautiful, resourceful…. want me to go on?"

"No, let's take these back to the boat so Hank can start using them and hopefully that pain in the ass Chewning has moved on."

When they got back, her wish was granted as Chewning was nowhere in sight but neither was Hank. Bones was onboard with his chamois drying the washdown.

"Where did everyone go?" asked Calhoun

"Hank has gone to the Red Lion with the dolphin and left-over conch for Woody to cook up. He walked out with Agent Chewning. I'm just finishing up but I'm beginning to wonder why I bothered washing it down looking at those clouds building over to the south of us. Storm is coming."

Calhoun and Eva had been so engrossed in their doggie bowl creations they had not noticed the change in the weather.

"Here, Bones" Eva said as she tossed one of the makeshift bowls to the first mate. "Take this home and use it to feed some of these poor animals and tell your friends to make some as well. There are too many dogs and too few scraps for them all so we need to look after them. Now, I'm going below to shower before dinner. And Calhoun, since you did such a good job in helping me, would you care to join me?"

The twinkle in her eye could not be missed and neither could an invitation like this.

"I am right behind you" came the reply as they both headed to the master stateroom. Bones could only shake his head in silent amusement as he made his way home with his makeshift bowl.

What none of them could appreciate at that moment was on that day an entire movement was born. Coconuts continued to be hollowed out and used as bowls for the strays on the island. As more transients came and went on their boats to fish the waters off Bimini, they too became caught up in saving the strays. In fact, the locals ended up painting coconuts with various scenes, generating keepsakes and creating their very own cottage industry. Within the fishing community, the effort became known as **E**very **V**essel **A**ssists or EVA in tribute to the creator. Eventually, they were able to fly a vet over from time to time to help try and manage the dog population through spay and neutering.

The metamorphosis of Eva from fun loving girl to fun loving woman had begun.

Chapter Fourteen

By the time Eva and Calhoun had finished their shower, the wind had come up, signaling the beginning of the storm. The sky had dramatically shifted from slate grey to pitch black. Hank, Calhoun and Eva were nearly bent over double, fighting the wind, as they made their way to the Red Lion accompanied only by the occasional splat of oversized raindrops hitting the cobblestone road.

Woody had just finished seating a large party of eight leaving only the bar as a place to sit which they gladly accepted. "Woody, I think we may go a bit off script tonight. How about a round of beers?" asked Calhoun.

Being the consummate barkeeper as well as restauranteur, three bottles of St. Pauli's Girl instantly appeared. Calhoun tilted the neck of his bottle toward his two companions "To better days!" "To better days!" came the response in unison.

Eva took a long pull from her beer, twirling her bottle in the process as she read the label.

"You know Calhoun, I have always been amused by their slogan, 'You Never Forget Your First Girl'. Very clever. All I can tell you is that you better never forget your last girl…me!"

"Eva, I don't think that will ever be possible." They both grinned liked two teenagers experiencing their first crush. All Hank could do was sit there and roll his eyes.

About fifteen minutes later a table came open so they adjourned to it where Woody had once again outdone himself preparing conch chowder with Bimini bread as an opener followed by grilled mahi with a light mango salsa and red rice covered in Hanks black beans, the latter using a recipe the captain had shared with Woody. Dessert was a locally made coconut ice cream.

Calhoun pushed back from the table declaring the meal one of the best he ever had while he filled the bowl of his pipe with fresh tobacco. Firing up the pipe he shared his thoughts. "I think it's smart we did not tell Chewning we were staying at the Big Game Club tonight. Let him post someone at the Mahalo, although I feel sorry for whoever draws that duty in this weather. If Slayder is still out there, he may think we are all tucked away on the boat."

"I have asked Bones to come back tonight to help stand watch just in case we do have a visitor. I had also asked him to prepare an overnight bag for you guys so you don't need to worry about that." Hank slid a key across the table toward Eva. "Room number 831."

"Wait! How did you get a key? We have all been together."

"I have my ways." responded the broadly smiling captain. "Now I suggest we get out of here before the deluge sets in."

They said their goodbyes at the door after thanking Woody for his extraordinary culinary skills and all set off at a trot, trying to avoid the promised monsoon.

Chapter Fifteen

They had no sooner reached their door than the heavens opened up in a torrent. Quickly ducking in, they saw the room held a pair of twin beds with a window unit air conditioner.

"Oh no!" admonished Eva to no one. "We are not sleeping in separate beds. We never have and I do not intend to start now." She immediately picked up the bedside phone which was directly connected to the front desk. She lodged her complaint to the desk clerk only to be informed there were no more rooms available.

"Great, just great!" she pouted as she hung up the phone. "No rooms. Looks like it will be tight quarters for us tonight."

Calhoun emerged from the bathroom brushing his teeth. "Surely we can make it through one night." he offered.

"Nope. One night turns to two and then three and suddenly we no longer share a bed. Not happening. Besides," she said patting the bed beside where she sat, "I have plans for you."

"But the shower…"

"That was then, this is now. Come here", she continued, patting the mattress beside her. As Calhoun sat down, she turned to face him. "Why do you think Slayder is so relentless? He doesn't give up."

Calhoun thought for a minute before replying. "I believe he is the type of person who wants to possess everything but own nothing." Calhoun continued. "He also has a maniacal obsession with you."

Eva thought on that statement for a moment then said, "Okay, I guess I can see that. Now would you mind turning on the AC before you get into bed. It's stuffy in here."

Calhoun walked over to the window and when he turned on the window unit, he was met with a sound similar to a jet engine starting up, a large whine which got increasingly louder until the desired temperature was reached. When the unit finally reached that temperature it shut down, sounding every bit like a transmission dropping from a car. All night this unique rhythm of the unit whining and thumping kept on. The only thing louder was the gale roaring outside. Eventually, after their first frolic in a single bed, they finally fell asleep but not before placing Calhoun's pipe and watch on the bedside table along with Eva's watch. Their sleep was long and deep as they embraced each other throughout the storm.

Eva awoke with a start not sure what had caused her to awaken. There was daylight leaking through the curtains but she was unsure of the time. She could tell the rain had stopped but the wind was still blowing hard. Without further opening her eyes, she felt around on the nightstand for one of the two watches she knew were there. Her hand came away with nothing which caused her to sit up. The bedstand was empty of their belongings.

"Calhoun, wake up!" the urgency in her voice brought him fully awake.

"What is it?"

"Our watches and your pipe are missing." By this time, Eva had swung her legs out of the bed and was looking under the table. "They are not here!"

Immediately Calhoun got up and checked the door to their unit. The door was locked but the safety chain was not engaged as it had been when they went to bed.

"Shit! I think someone has been in here." He circled the room with no success and finally walked into the bathroom stopping abruptly at the door. There, on the vanity, lay all of their things, laid out the way they had placed them on the nightstand the night before.

He grabbed them and turned to show Eva. It took only one look before she proclaimed, "That's it! We are going home and I mean going home today, like right now. Go find Chewning and get our passports back!"

The look in her eye and the tone in her voice told Calhoun all he needed to know. There was to be no further discussion, no compromise. The decision, her decision, was final.

Chapter Sixteen

The salon doors slammed open with such velocity it startled both Hank and Bones who were enjoying a cup of coffee together after having stood watch all night.

"What the hell?" was Hank's reaction as Eva stormed into the salon.

"Hank, we are leaving and we are leaving as soon as Calhoun gets back with everyone's passports." It was more of a command than a request.

"Have you noticed the winds out there? Seas are running six feet or better. We will get beat to death trying to cross now."

"Better than waiting on Slayder or one of his lackeys to do us harm." Eva quickly recounted the events from the previous evening leaving out the more intimate details.

No sooner had she finished than Calhoun came in with Agent Chewning in tow.

"I have been brought up to speed on what occurred last night and don't blame you for wanting to leave. I cannot in good conscience keep you here so Mr. Hipp has everyone's passports although crossing in this weather is ill advised I would think."

"Ill-advised or not, we are leaving and there is no room for discussion," informed Eva to the group of men. "I only have one question. How did someone get into our room with it locked and a security chain in place?"

Agent Chewning responded while shaking his head. "Sadly, anyone could have a master key around here. Security is not usually an issue on these islands. And as far as the chain goes, you can defeat those with not much more than a rubber band if you know what you are doing."

Hank apprised the situation now facing him. "We have enough fuel to get home so that is not a problem. We need to secure everything that is not tied down so Bones please inspect everything outside and then come back in to the main cabin and do a walk through in here. Then break out the foul weather gear for everyone. We can expect this weather to add at least another hour to our trip so be ready for that."

With that, everyone dispersed to get ready for the crossing with Agent Chewning wishing them good luck as he departed. Forty-five minutes later they were ready to depart, all of them clad in their bright yellow foul weather gear which served not only to keep them dry but to help spot them in case someone went overboard. Bones said his goodbyes and wished them well. He was glad he was not making the trip, given the wind outside. Hank had radioed to Miami Coast Guard informing them of their departure and in essence filing a float plan in case they went overdue into Ft. Lauderdale. A float plan was just like a flight plan for aircraft the difference being it was on the water rather than in the air.

Hank started the engines, secured the lines which had held the Mahalo at its berth and headed toward the jetties and out to sea. It was just shortly after ten a.m.

Chapter Seventeen

An angry and roaring ocean met them as they cleared the relative calm provided by the Bimini jetties. Instantly, the Mahalo was thrown into one of the most turbulent seas Hank had ever encountered during his career as a captain. They went 'skiing' down the top of one wave to hit the bottom of the trough only to be met by a great wall of water breaking over the bow of the boat and soaking everything in its path, including the flying bridge where Hank fought to keep the bow pointed directly into the waves attacking them. The up and down motion, coupled with the violent side to side rocking provided for a miserable ride. And no one was more aware of that than Eva who tried desperately to find some sanctuary somewhere on the boat. Her stomach was beginning to churn and she knew what would happen if she could not find somewhere where the wave action was not so dramatic.

She went down to the master stateroom to lie down. Actually, she curled up into a ball on the bed hoping to let the nausea pass. She was just about to drift off to sleep when something wet slapped across her face. She looked up and was horrified to see the portholes were leaking. The violence of the sea had somehow managed to penetrate the seals around these small openings. She knew she had to act. She immediately moved the mattress which lay beneath the leaks and went to the bathroom to secure as many towels as she could, laying them out beneath the openings in the hope they would absorb the water coming in. It was not much more than a trickle but it was a steady trickle which could add up over the course of the trip.

If it was leaking here, the other two staterooms were probably leaking as well so she went to both to find they were indeed getting wet. She then moved mattresses in both staterooms and lined the area underneath those portholes with all the towels she could find. The Mahalo was in no danger from this water intrusion. It was more a matter of inconvenience and it also eliminated a place where she could find some refuge from the storm. She began to wonder if she had not been too hasty in her decision to leave. They were only forty-five minutes into the trip and her doubts were already creeping in.

She was a decisive woman and her mind was made up so she knew she would just have to suck it up. She did realize that the activity of waterproofing all of the staterooms had made her nausea abate for the time being. She headed up to the main salon to see if the she could get comfortable there.

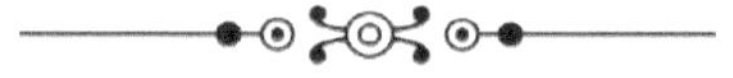

Chapter Eighteen

The main salon was not much better. She lay on the built-in sofa bed but the constant up and down motion accompanied by the occasional sideways slide down a wave only served to feed her nausea. She felt closed in. She needed fresh air.

Looking out the salon doors, she saw Calhoun, seemingly impervious to the wave action, sitting in one of the fighting chairs smoking his pipe. How could he be so immune to the roller coaster ride they were on?

Gathering her balance as best she could, she slid open the salon doors and holding onto to any surface which gave her purchase, she crabbed her way to the other fighting chair and sat down with a heavy thump.

"How are you feeling Eva?" he inquired. "I noticed you have been moving about a bit. You know this is the lowest point on the boat so it gets the least amount of wave action. You ought to sit here for a while. Might make you feel better."

She looked over at him in amazement. How could he sit here and not feel sick? The combination of rocking, along with the intermingled smell of diesel fumes and pipe tobacco put her over the edge.

She leapt up and leaned over the transom just in time as she lost the contents of her stomach in two retching's. She sat back on her haunches for a moment, trying to gather herself.

"I feel better now." She reported. "I'm going topside to check on Hank. Be back in a minute."

Calhoun watched her as she carefully climbed the ladder to the flying bridge. Once Hank saw her, he gave her a steadying hand and pulled her up the balance of way.

"What brings you up here?" Hank asked as Eva plopped down on the cushions surrounding the bridge.

"I just wanted to feel better and thought I would try here since I have pretty much been all over the boat with no relief. "

"Well, you will get more air here but it is also the highest point on the boat so you feel the rocking motion a lot more." He informed her.

"How much longer?" came a familiar refrain.

"We have been at it about ninety minutes so I would guess another three hours. I warned you this would not be easy but we should see the seas calm a bit as we get closer to Lauderdale. Hang in there." Which was all the encouragement Hank could offer.

And so, she did.

Chapter Nineteen

It was right at three p.m. when the Mahalo finally hit the mile buoy just outside the jetties leading into Ft. Lauderdale. Normally, this area was known as "Sailfish Alley" but today it was literally shelter from the storm as the seas dropped to a more customary two to three feet. Eva was exhausted but she had finally found some relief by curling into a ball on the main salon floor. Calhoun, for the most part, never left his fighting chair and seemed immune from the passage they had just undertaken. Nevertheless, he was glad to be back stateside.

Hank maneuvered the Mahalo into the gas docks at Pier 66 where they topped off the fuel tanks with diesel while waiting on Customs to clear them into the U.S. Forty-five minutes later had them squared away on both fronts and rounding the bend heading toward their permanent berth at slip F-142.

As they got closer to their slip, Hank noticed someone waving frantically at them and apparently yelling although he could not make out what she was saying over the hum of the engines.

"Hey, Eva" he yelled down to the cockpit where both she and Calhoun were sitting. "Do you know this gal?"

Having almost fully recovered from her crossing this morning, she scrambled up the ladder to the bridge followed closely by Calhoun.

She took one look and broke into a huge smile followed by a confused look of concern creasing her brow.

"That's my first cousin. I wonder why she is here."

Calhoun took one look and then glanced over to Hank who was showing a similar expression of confusion. For the gal standing on the dock in her halter top and short shorts waving so frantically and smiling so broadly was an exact twin to Eva, only as a brunette.

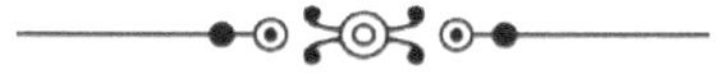

Chapter Twenty

"Brooke! What are you doing here?" Eva screamed in delight as she jumped off the boat and onto the dock even before Hank had secured the Mahalo.

"Well, Matt and I are going on a cruise that leaves later today from Port Everglades and since it is almost across the Causeway from here, I thought I would drop by to see if I could catch you. I was just leaving when I saw you guys come around the bend. I would love to see your boat."

"Of course, you can." Eva welcomed her cousin. "Calhoun, this is Brooke, we are first cousins. Her dad and my dad are brothers."

"Brooke, welcome aboard. I can't help but notice you and Eva are eerily twin like."

"Yeah, we got that a lot growing up. We are only four days apart in our birthdays and we lived next door to each other so we grew up more as sisters but everyone back home thinks we are like that Patty Duke TV show with identical cousins. So cuz, what am I looking at?"

For someone who had been so sick just a couple of hours ago, Eva warmed immediately to her new role as tour guide. "Well, when you step off the dock you will be stepping down into the cockpit. Those two chairs, or fighting chairs, are where we sit when catching fish. That ladder on the side goes up to the bridge, where Hank or Bones steer the boat and it also gives them a better view of the baits. These long pole like thingamyjimmies are the outriggers where the lines from the fishing rods go. Come on down and I will show you the inside where the main salon is and the galley or kitchen as you would call it and below that the sleeping area. Besides, you need to meet Hank who has disappeared somewhere in there."

Hank was emerging from the inferno created in the engine room after running for most of the day. Even though his gauges showed everything within normal parameters, nothing could replace the eyes on approach. Besides, he liked to check the oil dip sticks personally especially after a rough crossing.

"Come on Brooke. Let's go upstairs and visit," offered Eva.

"I wish I could but I left Matt at the Elbow Room. He wanted to visit with his old classmate, Chief. I need to go grab him and head over to

Carnival for our seven-day adventure. If I don't go now, Lord knows what kind of trouble they could get themselves into

"What time is your departure?" Eva pressed.

"Not until seven."

"Great!" Calhoun now stepped in. "We have time for you to tell me all about this young bundle of dynamite I seem to have become enamored with. Besides, Matt will be just fine visiting with his friend."

Seeing no way out, Brooke sat down on the main salon sofa bed and asked for a rum and Coke. She could tell this might take a while.

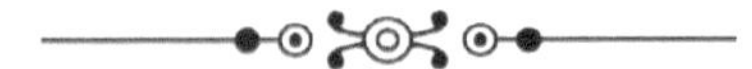

Chapter Twenty-One

"As I said, we are only four days apart as far as birthdays are concerned. And we did grow up next door to one another but it really wasn't next door. Well, the driveways were next to each other but our homes were on opposite sides of the ranches where we were raised so I guess there were at least fifty acres between the houses. When we were little we would try and ride our bikes to each other's places but the trails were overgrown and made it tough. And what the heck, we were raised on horse farms so by the time we were six or so we would just saddle up and go visit one another.

Now I gotta tell you. Miss Eva over here was a go getter. If she set her mind to something it was as good as done and with those looks…nobody denied her anything!"

Calhoun glanced at Eva who was slowly turning crimson. He tried to break the awkwardness by telling Brooke he bet she was quite the charmer as well.

"Nah, I was a late bloomer and by the time I was ready to court, Eva already had every guy in the county locked up tight for just her. That's one of the reasons Uncle Peter sent her off to school…too many hound dogs sniffing around his baby girl to suit him. But Lord knows, that didn't slow her down. I remember one Christmas Break when she was back home. She had found two wigs, one blonde and one brunette. We went to a Christmas party as each other, me in a blonde wig and her in the darker one. I can tell you that living just one night as her was exhausting, what with all the guys fawning all over me. But it really was nothing but good clean fun.

Anyway, she was what we called worldly…travelling everywhere, meeting people. We all knew she would go places until she fell into the wrong crowd. Calhoun, there are a bunch of people back in Georgia who sure would like to thank you for rescuing their pride and joy."

"Believe me Brooke, she rescued me even more so." He only took two steps to cross over the space between where he had been standing and where Eva now sat and wrapped an arm around her shoulders. "I'm just blessed she came into my life." Eva looked up at him and it was apparent to all that a great love flowed between the two of them.

"Well, I hate to break the spell but I gotta go." declared Brooke. "If I don't get over to the Elbow Room, and grab Matt, he won't be worth shooting. Lord only knows what he and Chief have been up to!"

With the requisite goodbyes said, Brooke headed back toward her car leaving Hank, Calhoun and Eva on the boat.

"Captain, tomorrow let's meet and come up with a plan for the next few weeks. In the meantime, Eva and I are going back to the condo and I, for one, am going to shower and hit the rack"

"Not without me you won't" chimed in the only female voice left on the boat. "Your plan, Calhoun, sounds delicious!"

And indeed, it turned out just that way.

Chapter Twenty-Two

They all reconvened the next day on board the Mahalo at ten a.m. Calhoun and Eva had managed to sleep in a while at their Bahia Mar condo and even got in a morning stroll along the beach sans horseflies and other pests which seemed to trail them in Bimini.

Hank had been working on a list and got right to the point.

"Mr. Hipp, I think we are overdue to have the boat pulled out, the bottom scrapped of barnacles and repainted, the engines tuned because they are getting up there in the hours on them and candidly, we could use some updated electronics such as a new fish finder, sonar and radio equipment. Plus, I would suggest we pull the eight-track player and replace it with a cassette tape deck…those tapes are smaller and thus don't take up as much room as the eight tracks." With that, Hank handed the list to Calhoun who studied it for a few moments.

"I can't really fault anything you have listed here. It's not going to be cheap based on the estimates you have. How soon could you get started?"

"As a matter of fact, I've called the shipyard in New Bern, North Carolina and they can jump right on this as soon as I can ferry the boat up there. That should take me eight to ten days to run it up staying mostly in the Intercostal Waterway. I also have a buddy, Captain Stank Wood, who you guys met in Bimini. He has to go up there to pick up a boat so he will accompany me on the way up and I will help him with his boat coming back. That works out pretty well as we can run some at night and shorten the trip. With your permission, we can leave tomorrow."

"Let's do it. Besides, I need to get back to Greenville for a few days. As you know, I have a birthday coming up and a couple of friends want to throw a small get together for me. It's awfully kind but I would be fine without the fuss. Also, they have reminded me I have kept Eva pretty much hostage with me since some have only met her once and others have not yet met her at all and it's been over three years of dating. I will have the company plane pick us up tomorrow as well and we will stay in Greenville until the boat is ready."

Hank nodded and replied, "Give me thirty days and I will give you back an updated and almost new boat."

Calhoun looked over to Eva. "You okay with this schedule?" he asked.

"Let's do it." was her quick reply.

Chapter Twenty-Three

The next day at six a. m. found Hank pacing back and forth on the dock waiting on his associate Stank Wood. Never known for his promptness, it still frustrated Hank as he knew they had a long eight days in front of them. He was thinking about his timetable and where to overnight when his reverie was interrupted.

"Henry! Let's get going!" Another thing Hank hated was to be called by his given name. The only person to do it was Stank and that was only allowed because of their long-time friendship. Hank looked up to see his friend bounding across the mini golf course separating the parking lot from the docks. With a go bag in hand, an unlit cigar clamped between his teeth and a mustachioed grin on his face he looked every bit the riverboat gambler he was known to be.

"Whatcha waiting on Cap?" came a totally rhetorical question.

"You, as always." responded Hank as he ascended the ladder going up to the flying bridge and started the engines. "Now get those lines off, store your things and bring me a cup of coffee!"

A quick hand salute, overly involving his middle finger was all the acknowledgement Hank needed to know that Stank had gotten the message. Hank knew the next eight days would be a challenge, not only from a transit standpoint, but with the reputation of Stank. His fellow captain and friend had never met a deck of cards or a bottle of Dewars he didn't like and there would be plenty of both awaiting their journey once word got out that Captain Wood was heading their way. A lot of Captains had lost money to this rogue and they always were in wait at a chance to get some of it back. They would, inevitably, fail.

Hank's plan was to try and get as far as Amelia Island tonight. Tomorrow they would run outside the Intracoastal, better known as 'the ditch' to most. He would try for Savannah from that waypoint which would cut off about eighty miles from their trip. Cruising at his planned sixteen knots would allow them to make the covered docks of the City Marina in Charleston with no problem the following day. This was basically his entire float plan, hopscotching all the way up the east coast until they arrived in New Bern.

Moments later, Stank arrived on the bridge with two steaming mugs of coffee in hand. "Should be a good run" he commented. "Weather looks like it will hold and there are plenty of guys who want a piece of me as we move up the coast. Should be a profitable trip. By the way, where did your owners head off to?"

"Greenville" replied Hank.

"South Carolina?"

"Yeah, that Greenville."

Chapter Twenty-Four

Greenville, S.C.

When Calhoun had sold his home in order to move to Florida on a more permanent basis, he had retained possession of the two-bedroom, two bath guesthouse adjacent to the main house. This is where the two newly arrived travelers now found themselves.

"Calhoun, I can't believe I never came over here the one time I came to Greenville but I guess everything was such a whirlwind I just lost track. This is perfect for our needs." Eva was perusing his small library of books as she spoke, eventually settling on the definitive works of Dante.

"Dante? Really Eva?" Calhoun could not help but notice the book she had just pulled from the shelf.

"Why not? There is more to me than you may realize." While this last statement was not delivered in defiance, Calhoun knew he was on tricky ground. His young vixen was now growing into a more mature version and he liked what he saw.

"So, let's plan out the next few weeks. Hank says the boat will be ready in about thirty days. Aside from the party RAM wants to give, do you have anything else you would like to do?" Calhoun hoped he was not being too obvious by the sudden topic change.

"We are here at the foothills to the Blue Ridge Mountains so I would like to go drive and see them. It will give me a chance to possibly dust off my painting skills which have taken second fiddle to a whole bunch of sportfishing. I'm not complaining but I would like to do a couple of oil on canvas drawings if the chance comes up.

Now, let's talk about RAM. What a strange name and in all caps?"

"RAM is my friend, Robert Alonso MacIntire. He never liked his name so he decided back in college just to go by RAM and it has stuck, even down to the all caps. He is a consultant, whatever that means, because he never seems to be doing anything but he can find anything you need. I half believe he is with the CIA because he is so mysterious but so resourceful at the same time. He and his wife Twazie are hosting my supposed birthday party tomorrow night and all we have to do is show up at seven."

"Perfect. Tomorrow I want to go to an arts and crafts store to buy supplies and then the day after, we picnic and paint. It will be nice to continue to be out of the humidity for awhile and the green outdoors will be a welcomed change of pace. And now I am going to sit out on the porch and dig into my latest literary find" she trumpeted proudly holding up her book on Dante.

"And I am going to lay down and take a nap," countered Calhoun. "Later this evening I will take you into town to Charlie Spivak's for a decent steak and great music."

"I like the way you think," came the already distracted reply.

Chapter Twenty-Five

It was six-thirty the next evening. Calhoun and Eva were getting close to RAM's home after a full day of shopping and a bit of sightseeing for Eva.

"So, tell me more about RAM other than this man of mystery."

"Nothing much more I can add. I met him years ago at a party. We became friends, especially once I learned how resourceful he was. Other than that, I will let you come to your own conclusions. And you can start doing that right now because here we are!"

Calhoun pulled his convertible Mercedes into the driveway of a three-story Victorian-Gothic styled home. Painted a deep crimson, giving the appearance of dried blood, the dwelling looked straight out of a Charles Addams cartoon. And on the wraparound porch stood two figures who would look comfortable in such a drawing.

Eva took in the entire scene and could only utter a muted "Oh my."

"Told you to come to your own conclusions" smiled Calhoun as he got out of his car and walked around the side to open the door for Eva. She was dressed in her Peter Max dress which Calhoun had purchased for her sometime back and was her favorite outfit. Paired with what she referred to as her Go-Go Boots, she was dressed to kill and Calhoun wondered how his conservative friends would react.

"You look stunning, as always" he remarked as she unlimbered from the car exposing a lot more leg than he was comfortable with.

"And you look great as well in your navy blazer and Khaki pants. The golf shirt may be a bit casual but who cares? After all it's YOUR birthday party."

"Mr. Palm Beach!" roared RAM as he caught sight of Calhoun. "Looking good son what with the blazer, golf shirt, alligator loafers' sans socks. Bringing new style to Greenville!" RAM continued to yell as though everyone around him was deaf. He bounded off the porch, all five foot five inches of him, almost rolling down the steps just like the bowling ball he resembled. "And you, my child must the lady who stole his heart" giving a slight bow from the waist while kissing the back of her hand.

"And Eva, this is my wife Twazie" pointing to the porch where Twazie remained. Eva glanced up and was shocked to see a rail thin woman standing there. Eva's first thought was this woman makes Twiggy look like she needs to diet and her second thought was if she turns sideways, she will all but disappear. Then Eva quickly admonished herself for such thoughts, dismissing them by saying, "Twazie, it is nice to meet you finally. I have heard so much about you and RAM. We really appreciate you hosting Calhoun's birthday party at such a unique venue." This last statement made her shudder as the home itself was nothing less than creepy.

"Come in and make yourselves at home" offered Twazie as she turned to go back inside, literally disappearing in the process which caused Eva to shudder a second time.

Chapter Twenty -Six

As far as cocktails parties went, this one was about as mundane as they get. Oh, sure, the people Eva met were kind enough but for many this was their first time in her presence and the sideways glances or outright stares belied their curiosity. The drinks were plentiful and the food scarce as it was apparent RAM had placed the majority of his budget on the bar side of this event. Two very nice gentlemen, John and Joe held court at the one bar RAM had set up, plying their trade as world class mixologists as well as being a fountain of knowledge on the goings on of Greenville. Eva found herself hanging around them more than anyone else as she got more information on Greenville in general and Calhoun in particular from these two gentlemen.

RAM worked the crowd where an occasional roar of laughter would erupt over some off-color story he was telling while Twazie flitted about making sure the canapes plate stayed full and emptying the overflowing ashtrays as needed.

Every time Eva caught sight of her, she seemed to be disappearing back into the bowels of the home, presumably into the kitchen area. Eva wished she could grab her for conversation as she was curious about the crowd, but the chance never came.

Finally, a little before nine, RAM rolled out a cake, shaped in the form of the Mahalo featuring a scantily clad girl on the bow which undoubtably was his take on Eva. With an exaggerated number of candles occupying every available space, RAM led the group in a horribly off-key rendition of Happy Birthday as Calhoun had to act as a human bellows in order to put out the miniature inferno RAM had created.

Before the cake could be cut, the hallway grandfather clock started chiming out the nine o'clock hour. As Eva watched in fascination, Joe and John started clearing the bar, Twazie grabbed the cake cart and began rolling it toward the kitchen and RAM disappeared around the corner. Their actions were so sudden, Eva wondered if they were rehearsed.

She had just made her way back to Calhoun, looping her arm through his when they all were assailed by a loud whirring noise.

Eva looked up at Calhoun and said, "Please tell me that is not what I think it is."

“I’m afraid so.”

Those words had barely escaped Calhoun’s lips when RAM rounded the corner with a vacuum cleaner going full blast as he started to move people out of the way by pushing it in front of and indeed over the feet of people who may be standing in his way.

Eva did not even try to disguise her amusement as she laughed out loud at the improbable antics of their host.

“I guess that means the party is over,” she said giving Calhoun a quick kiss on his cheek and laughing even louder as she caught the bemused shock on his face. “Let’s go. RAM is calling the party; I’ve met a lot of nice people who love you dearly and besides I have my own present to give you when we get home.”

The twinkle in those other worldly green eyes and the deep-set dimples, all of which Calhoun had come to adore, gave him some idea as to what she had in mind.

He was not disappointed.

Chapter Twenty-Seven

"Five days!" The exasperation in Eva's voice was clear. Her frustration was evident as she stood overlooking the fog shrouded valley below her. She had scouted a place to paint a couple of days after the vacuum party as she called it. Boy, that had been a tough thank you note to write! But now, her painting plans were put on hold for yet another day.

"Not much we can do about the weather Eva other than wait it out."

"I know Calhoun but as I told you I only have a couple of hours each day when the lighting is right and now this valley will not let go of this blanket of fog. It's held on for nearly a week. Besides, I am so looking forward to a day of painting and picnicking. But I guess we will return to your cabana where I can continue my reading of Dante and you can lay by the pool. Tomorrow is going to be a better day…I just feel it!"

And she was right, as the next day bloomed clear and bright and free of any low-lying clouds. Now Eva could barely contain her excitement as they drove the road down into this valley located in the foothills of the Blue Ridge Mountains.

"Stop! Pull over!" she yelled, startling Calhoun in the process. "This is the place." It was her artists eye that had now taken over. They were on a switchback on the mountain road, not the safest place to stop but just at their feet was the beginning of a trail which appeared large enough to handle their car. The trail was all but invisible as most people were busy navigating the mountain road and were often past this point before realizing they had even arrived. Calhoun allowed the car to meander down the makeshift roadway until Eva indicated it was time to stop. Looking over the scene which stretched in front of her she announced their arrival.

Her head on a swivel, she slowly turned three hundred and sixty degrees, taking in the panoramic view in its entirety. "Yep, this is it." They were on a small rise, giving an unobstructed view of the valley below while simultaneously shielding them from view from the mountain road above them.

In no time she had emptied the trunk of her painting supplies and had set up her easel. She first took a pad and sketched the scene in front of her to better give her the perspective she wanted. She immediately began mixing her paints to give her the hues she was looking for and with a bit of trepidation she started very gingerly painting the background.

"You amaze me." observed Calhoun. "I never knew you painted until this trip."

Without looking at him but keeping her eyes riveted to the scene in front of her she responded. "We never had a chance on Bimini as things were just a bit frantic but I minored in art when I was in college. Now just watch and let me concentrate."

Eva worked at a practiced pace for the next two and a half hours before the sun had moved out of position casting long shadows into the valley in front of them.

"That's it for the day." She announced. "Now, Calhoun help me get these art supplies put away and let's get out the picnic."

The day remained nothing less than glorious as they spread a blanket on the grassy rise where just moments earlier Eva had been busy at work. Various meats, cheeses, bread and grapes appeared, taking the place of the paint brushes and oils. Calhoun managed to even pop a bottle of chilled chardonnay much to the delight of Eva.

There wasn't much conversation as they reveled being in each other's company. They lingered over their meal with Calhoun stretching out, folding his hands behind his head as he became drowsy from the effects of the wine.

"On no mister." A gleeful and suddenly playful Eva commanded. "You are not going to sleep on me. There is still dessert!"

"I didn't bring anything for dessert." replied a crestfallen Calhoun.

"Well, I did."

"And what might that be?" queried a suddenly wide-awake Calhoun who had an idea where this was going.

"Kisses and cuddles of course."

"I think I may like this dessert."

And indeed, he did.

Chapter Twenty-Eight

For the next four days, Calhoun marveled as the scene in front of him was magically transferred to the canvas Eva worked over. She started with the background capturing the pale blue sky and the lone finger of a cumulus cloud and worked diligently as the sky merged with the mountains and then onto the valley below with just a hint of the fogbank that had haunted her earlier in the week as her tribute to Mother Nature. This may have not been the most orthodox way to attack a painting, but what would you expect when dealing with Eva? Every painting session lasted around two hours before the light faded culminating with a picnic and then Eva's special dessert. Later in the week, she added in a roof top that did not actually exist there but explained to Calhoun she liked Scandinavian style architecture so in it went along with a smattering of Italian Cypress trees "just because she liked them". There was a church steeple in the distance which she also captured. On the one Sunday they were painting, they were regaled with the sounds of the church bells no doubt summoning those who lived in what Calhoun envisioned was the village it served. The forest prevented them from seeing any other structures. However, one thing puzzled him. The foreground of the scene was blank, leaving the bottom quarter of the canvas untouched.

"Why the blank space?" he asked on the fifth day of painting as he tapped out the tobacco in the bowl of his pipe in preparation to fire up a fresh bowl.

"I have a special plan for that."

"And?"

"And that includes you. See that field of wild dandelions over there? You are going to insert those into the foreground. I want this to be a painting we both worked on."

"I have no artistic ability."

"You have more than you know. Now watch."

She quickly dabbed colors of white with spots of yellow depicting the flowers.

"Now your turn."

He took the brush from her hand and tried to imitate her actions. He was far more deliberate as he lacked the confidence and skill that Eva possessed but as the minutes wore on, he got the hang of it and his confidence grew.

"I told you that you had more ability than you gave yourself credit for."

"It's all due to you and the faith you had in me." He leaned in to give her a kiss and finished with dabbing her nose with his paint brush.

"You'll pay for that mister! Now let's get this cleaned up and put away. We should be finished with this project by tomorrow or no later than the next day. In fact, I want to take the painting to the boat as I have the perfect spot in mind as to where we can hang it. Right over our bed to remind me of this place and our special time together."

Calhoun was so touched by her comment that he leaned in for another kiss. But it ended up being much more than just that.

Chapter Twenty-Nine

Two days later they had finished their painting well before the sun had surrendered its light, which found them heading back to Calhoun's bungalow earlier than usual. When he had kept this house, he had also kept two parking spaces in front of it, slightly to the right of the now sold colonial styled main home. When they pulled up the driveway, they were surprised to see at least half a dozen vehicles parked haphazardly around the parking area with some pulled up on the grass circle in front of the main home.

"Now what in the hell do you think this is all about?" voiced a concerned Eva.

"I don't know but I don't like it. Looking at some of these license tags, they appear to mostly belong to law enforcement."

"Well, this mystery isn't going to solve itself so let's go see what music we have to dance to. Maybe someone didn't like a weeks' worth of indecent exposure after our painting sessions!"

"Well, shame on them if that's the best this group can do!" Calhoun grabbed the canvas with their mutual work on it and along with Eva headed to their two-bedroom hideaway which had apparently failed in its purpose for it was hidden no more.

When they opened the front door, the crescendo of voices that had been trying to outduel themselves in volume, suddenly ceased, leaving an uncomfortable silence. Eva tried to survey the room to see who she recognized but the smoke encapsulated area, from eight men smoking, made it difficult to breathe and to see so she immediately ushered everyone out onto the porch where her shock became apparent once she identified who had come to this impromptu party.

The first person she saw was Agent Chewning along with two of his traveling companions. She also recognized the captain in charge of the Royal Bahamian Police for the district of Bimini. Mr. Holmes from the Big Game Club was there as well. But she had never been so excited as to see the next man walk outside…Bones. She could not suppress her delight or surprise as she ran to embrace him. However, that embrace proved to be short-lived as the last man out, shocked her to her core…. Bowers.

"What is he doing here?" the tenor of her voice leaving no doubt as to her total disdain.

Calhoun finally found his voice. "As a matter of fact, what in the hell are all of you doing here?"

Agent Chewning stepped forward. "Fair question which will take awhile to answer so why don't you two get comfortable and I'll explain."

Both Eva and Calhoun grabbed two of the Kennedy rockers they had on the porch, turned them to face the ensemble gathered in front of them when Calhoun simply said, "Begin."

Chapter Thirty

"Let me begin by saying we all apologize for this sudden intrusion." Agent Chewning stood directly in front of the still astonished couple.

"In the weeks since you all left Bimini, the drug trade has become increasingly more prevalent and with that, violence has also increased. We know it is due to Slayder but he still remains elusive as his little empire continues to expand."

"And you know this how?" spat Eva.

"Because I was the source of the information" volunteered Bowers.

"You? You traitor. How could anyone believe you? And why aren't you in jail where you belong?"

Bowers started to step forward but he was intercepted by Captain Shumate of the Bahamian Police. With a gently extended arm, he held Bowers back.

"I can explain that since it was my idea. I asked Bowers if he would go undercover for us.

Try to learn what he could, particularly as to Slayder's whereabouts and time tables. On the night you attended the dinner at the Anchors Aweigh, even Bowers was surprised when Slayder suddenly showed up at the Compleat Angler. He had no way to warn any of us…"

"But I can promise you I would never have allowed any harm to come to you." Bowers vehemently interjected.

Eva sat back, taking all this in. This new information made her head spin.

"Why the U.N. treatment?" asked Calhoun. "Aside from our Federal Government, it seems half the island is here. We are just missing Woody and Hank."

Captain Shumate responded once again. "Believe me, Woody wanted to be here to help convince you guys and Hank is on the way to pick up the overhauled Mahalo."

"Convince us to do what?" asked Eva in an uncertain tone as to what may come next.

Mr. Holmes now took center stage. "The annual Island Fishing Tournament is coming up in a few weeks. It is customary for the years previous champions to return to defend their title. As winning female angler, The Big Game Club officially extends that invitation to you with the hopes you can see your way clear to make a return trip."

Agent Holmes picked up the narrative. "We will publicize your return with the hopes this will draw out Slayder one more time. I can assure you that we will provide every protection necessary to safeguard your wellbeing. We need to shut Slayder's operation down for good and you, Eva, are our best chance to make that happen."

All the while, Calhoun had remained silent, almost contemplative. He took his time filling the bowl of his pipe, lighting it with a few long pulls before he addressed the men in front of him. "Gentlemen, it was no easy task for you to assemble this group to make this plea. I am impressed with what you have done and by those gathered here. I want one thing understood, Eva and I will not be free of Slayder until he is behind bars so we will help and we will fish. As long as two conditions are met. First, Eva agrees to every aspect of your plans and secondly, she is protected as well as any head of state. What do you say Eva?"

All eyes now turned to the green-eyed beauty. She appeared to be lost in thought as the moments ticked by. Finally, she looked at the assembled group.

"Deal."

With that one word a spontaneous cheer went out from the group.

"Now who the hell gave permission to Hank to go get my boat?" yelled Calhoun as everyone broke into laughter.

Part Two

Chapter Thirty-One

Calhoun sat on his balcony overlooking the Bahia Mar Marina, his pipe in its customary place, gritted tightly between his teeth, as a halo of tobacco smoke circled just above his head. He loved this view of all the boats and especially the cacophony of noise the sailboats made as their brass fittings and clips beat relentlessly against the aluminum masts in the gentle breeze.

It had been two days since the impromptu summit in Greenville. In that time Eva had managed to pack up the house and even get a temporary frame for their painting as she insisted on taking it with her. The Beechcraft King Air had whisked them down late yesterday afternoon. He basked in the warmth of the South Florida sun before it got too hot to enjoy.

Eva, having just taken a phone call, finally joined him. "That was Hank." she reported. "He got in late last night and is headed over here to give us an update."

"Hard to believe all that has happened in just forty-eight hours. It will be good to see Hank and I am anxious to see what they have done to my boat.

So, tell me Eva, what do you really think of this plan to finally put an end to this cat and mouse with Slayder now that you have had some time to reflect on it."

"Well, to paraphrase our late president, 'If not now, when; if not us, who?' I believe we are the best cheese in the trap and if he is ever going to be caught, this is the perfect time. Heck, the way they are touting the return of the defending champion anglers, how could I resist. I will be a celebrity on Bimini!"

"You already are with your apparent fishing prowess and now I hear your stray dog coconut bowl campaign has really take off." Eva took the compliments with restrained pride and let the moments soak in.

Before she could finally reply, the doorbell rang. Hank had arrived.

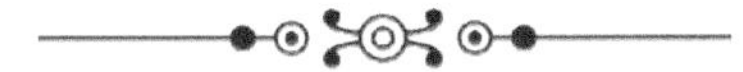

Chapter Thirty-Two

"Good Morning Everyone!" chirped an overly ebullient Hank. "You guys ready to get back to fishing?"

"Now aren't we the chipper one? Why the extra good mood Captain?" asked Eva.

"All I can say is the Mahalo is running as well as she did the day we initially took possession. The paint job and removal of barnacles off the bottom as well as tuning the engines has added a couple of knots to her top end speed which will help in a couple of weeks for the tournament. Her new electronics have lots of potential. In fact, I would like to try out the new fish finder tomorrow if you guys are up for a day of fishing. We have a title to defend and a crook to catch. You can tell I have been talking with Bones who brought me up to date on the Greenville meeting.

There are a couple of things you both need to know. It is no longer safe to travel to Bimini alone. Drug smugglers have been hijacking boats using fast boats or what they call cigarette boats to overtake their targets, setting the crew adrift if not outright killing them and using those captured boats for a one time only drug run before someone reports the boat missing. Usually, they come at dusk before the Coast Guard can put a helo in the air and they lose them in the darkness. They know they can outrun any cutter the Coast Guard has but they can't outrun a radio so darkness is their friend. But they are getting bolder in hijacking in broad daylight. Anyway, they usually abandon the boat in the swamp somewhere if they cannot outright scuttle it. So, we will need to make sure at least one other boat is traversing to Bimini at the same time because there is safety in numbers. Also, I will be bringing a shotgun with me to defend ourselves if we do run into a situation. You have met the captain of police over there and while it is illegal to bring a weapon into the country, the authorities are turning a blind eye to this until they can get the trafficking under control. Believe me, we will not be the only boat who will be bringing extra protection into Bimini for the near term."

Calhoun took an extra long pull on his pipe before he spoke. "I hate that it has come to this but I will not be intimidated by a bunch of thugs. I want to make sure Eva stays safe but from what you just said and the plan you have laid out, I believe we have taken every precaution we can. So, let's fish tomorrow and get back into tournament mode. When do we leave for Bimini?"

"In five days. We will be there for the welcoming party at the Big Game Club where we will be staying. So, if you guys are okay with everything, I'll see you tomorrow around eight at the dock. I have a boat to provision and set up so let me get going. Don't get up, I know the way out. Enjoy your day!"

"With all that you just dropped on us, that might be a challenge but you know we will find a way." Eva grinned back at the departing captain.

Chapter Thirty-Three

The next day, like so many in south Florida, dawned with clear skies and a gentle breeze coming from the south. In other words, a perfect day to fish, perhaps a little too flat from Hank's standpoint but nevertheless, ideal conditions.

Seven-thirty found both Calhoun and Eva at Slip F-142, the home slip for the Mahalo. Hank was already there, busy rigging baits and putting out rods.

"It looks to be a good day to knock the rust off you guys. I need to get you back into top angler shape if Eva is going to retain the crown. By the way, I was on the radio earlier with a captain friend of mine, LaRue Smickums. He tells me there are over fifty boats registered for this event. So many, they decided to close registration. After the Hanky Panky burned last year in the harbor, they are not going to allow any free anchorage during the tournament which means if you don't have a slip you are going to have to overnight at Cat Cay and fish out of there."

"Wait, wait, wait. Did you say you have a friend named LaRue Smickums? Really?" Eva was about to burst into laughter but was trying her utmost to keep her composure.

"Yeh, he's a pretty good captain when it comes to fishing. He is a native Charlestonian, both his parents being French Huguenots, thus the unusual name. Nevertheless, he will be some competition we didn't have last time we fished this tournament. You will know if he has a good day because he comes back to the dock singing all manner of show tunes. He does a pretty mean imitation of Elvis as well, especially after a few Rum Punches. The guys just usually roll their eyes but the women really do swoon. On nights like that he ends up catching more than just fish. Now enough idle chatter. Let's get those spring lines off and leave the stern line for last. I have another trick I want to show you once we get our fishing lines wet and I can't do that sitting here!"

Chapter Thirty-Four

"Keep that rod tip up! Jeez! Did you forget everything I taught you?"

The object of Hank's frustration was Eva. He intended to be especially hard on her as he wanted her reactions and muscle memory to be automatic. They had just gotten into a school of dolphin and as usual, Hank wanted to boat every one. Calhoun had already reeled in a seven pounder and was now relegated to spectator as he knew better than to get in the way of either Eva or Hank. Eva gave Hank a quick look and smile, her dimples clearly visible underneath the ballcap she wore.

"I got this captain" she announced. "I may be rusty but I am not a rookie!" And to prove her point she finished reeling in a nice twenty-two-pound bull dolphin. It was a nice size fish but it also cost them the school they were in as the rest of the dolphin broke off contact.

Hank was nonplussed over losing the school. Normally he would have been more frustrated but today he wanted to show both Calhoun and Eva his 'secret weapon'.

"You guys come up here to the bridge. I have a new rig I want to get you familiar with."

Once everyone was assembled, Hank pointed out one of the latest features he had installed. "As you can see, I have a rod holder attached to the handrail up here. From this point we are going to add a fifth line but just not any old line. This one will be dedicated to kite fishing." Holding up both his hands in the universal signal to stop, he continued. "Let me finish before you start with your questions. This rig will take the line from a rod that will be here and run it up the starboard outrigger where it will be attached to a kite trailing behind us. All you need to know is that the kite will give the bait additional energy looking more like a live bait. Plus, the only part of the line in the water will be coming down straight from the kite to the bait, no lines skimming the surface like we currently have. This will be line five and since it is positioned up here, tournament rules will allow me or Bones to grab it and hand it off to you. After that, Eva, you will have your work cut out for you. Noticed I said Eva. Sorry, boss, but if she is going to be a repeat champion, she needs to handle every opportunity she can. You will be sitting in second chair, basically adding to whatever she cannot get to."

"Questions?" Before she could open her mouth Hank interjected. "Good. Now Eva, get back to your fighting chair. Calhoun, I want you down there too. We are going to try this contraption out and if we catch anything I need to hand you the rod as seamlessly as possible and you can put it in the gimble on her chair. After that, you and I trade places."

It took a few minutes for Hank to get the kite rigged and flying but once he did, the bait jumped and danced all over the trailing wake of the Mahalo. Calhoun watched in silent amazement. This little add on might just win them a tournament. "Hank, you sure these are legal?" Before he could get a response, Hank was up and yelling "FIVE, FIVE, FIVE!"

All Calhoun could think was, legal or not, they sure seemed to work.

Chapter Thirty-Five

Hank grabbed the rod from the holder on the bridge and passed it down to Calhoun who immediately placed the rod in the gimble on Eva's fighting chair.

"Let her spool for a second" yelled Hank from the bridge. "Lower your rod…. wait…wait. NOW! Tighten the drag and pull back!"

Eva did as she was told and was instantly rewarded. As the kite danced back and forth without a bait attached, a sudden explosion erupted behind the Mahalo…a blue marlin shot up through the water as if it was trying to catch the kite. As it slammed back into the water on its side, cheers erupted from Calhoun who was the only spectator at the moment. Hank was focused on his quarry as was Eva, intent on keeping the line tight.

"Clean hook up Eva. You know what to do. Keep that line tight, bring the rod back slowly but steady and reel as you go down. Just like I taught you." The grin on Hank's face was matched with every grin on the Mahalo. They just might have the secret to winning a tournament and the bait to catch Slayder as well!

Chapter Thirty-Six

Two days later, a little bit ahead of their own self-imposed schedule, three boats set out from Ft. Lauderdale to Bimini. As soon as they cleared the jetties, the 45' Viking known as the Tedi Bare and captained by LaRue Smickems, took the lead with the Mahalo and Daddy's Girl following about 100 yards behind on either flank. This formation would allow them to close ranks rapidly, if need be, in the event they were approached by unknown boats.

"It feels very much like an old wagon train of past years." remarked Eva. "I just hope we don't see any Indians on our crossing. And you, my love, look every bit the part of a John Ford Western."

Calhoun was sitting next to her in the adjacent fighting chair. Draped across his lap, a la someone riding shotgun, was a 12-gauge shotgun with the plug removed allowing for extra shells. Hank was in his perch on the flying bridge, armed only with the flare gun which would serve a dual purpose if necessary. He could aim it heavenwards to send a distress flare or shoot it straight down into any boat attempting to come alongside causing a conflagration which he was confident would end any attempt to illegally board. Every boat, in this mini armada, was similarly armed.

"I'm glad we left earlier than our announced departure." Eva continued. "If Slayder has any ears over here they hopefully have relayed the wrong departure date in case they wanted to try something on the open seas."

It was at that moment Hank shimmed down the ladder from the bridge, binoculars swinging from his neck.

"I've been talking with the other two captains. Nothing to report as yet. Eva, why don't you go topside and keep watch. She is on autopilot so just keep looking at the horizon, all 360 degrees of it. And I'm also hesitant to report that while we may have a secret weapon for this tournament, Captain Smickums looks like he brought one as well. In fact, his is legendary amongst all of us captains so go take a peek at that while you are up there." With that he handed her the binoculars and disappeared into the main salon.

Eva scampered up to the bridge to take her overwatch position. It was less than five minutes later when she screamed, letting out a terrified shout, "WHAT IS THAT THING?"

Chapter Thirty – Seven

At the sound of sheer terror in Eva's voice, Calhoun threw the shotgun he had been cradling across the top of the fishbox, thankful that his action had not triggered some type of accidental discharge. He got up the ladder to the bridge in scant moments only to find the binoculars glued to Eva's face held with one hand and pointing shakily with her free hand at the Tedi Bare.

Without a word, he gently removed the binoculars from Eva's grip and trained them on the area that had caused her such panic. In the meantime, Hank had also rejoined them on the bridge but without any of the consternation displayed by his top angler or owner.

Without removing the glasses from the spot he was focused on, Calhoun asked "Hank, what am I looking at?"

Calhoun could tell from the tone in Hank's voice that he was having fun with them both.

"That, sir, is a Grand Cayman blue iguana you see perched on Captain LaRue's neck. He carries it into tournaments as his good luck charm. Rumor has it that if that animal sneezes while they are fishing, they are onto a fish. Kinda his early warning device. Like our kite, it's his secret weapon. He seldom loses when she is aboard."

"She?" queried Eva.

"Louise is her name to be exact. LaRue rescued her from the jaws of death as he plucked her from the ocean just as a Mako was about to make a snack out of her. She has been by his side ever since. Quite a sight to see her on a leash walking him to dinner down one of the docks.

"Exactly how big is that dinosaur?" Eva snapped as she turned and gave Hank a knowing look.

"Louise is about four feet long and weighs about twenty pounds. You can find her either around LaRue's neck or sitting on the back of his captain's chair."

"You knew, didn't you." Eva was in full attack mode. "You knew when you called me to the bridge I would see that thing. You set me up…. again. I swear Hank, one day I will get even with you if I can ever figure out how to just catch up!" She was smiling now as she knew she had been bested once again. Before Hank could respond, the radio crackled with LaRue's voice.

"Heads up! We've got company, everyone."

Chapter Thirty-Eight

ank immediately relieved Calhoun of the binoculars he was holding and grabbed for the boats microphone. "Where abouts Captain?"

"Dead straight ahead. I make out three fast boats. I've just called it into Miami Station. These guys are getting more brazen every day. Hell, we aren't even out of sight of the mainland yet. Everyone, tighten up on me and let's show them who they are dealing with!"

"10-4" came the responses from the Mahalo and Daddy's Girl as they both throttled up to tighten the distance between all three boats. If those guys on the other side tried anything, they would be met with a hail of gunfire.

"Calhoun, get back down into the fighting cockpit and Eva, get into the main salon." barked Hank whose tone told them there would be no discussion. He was the captain and this was now his boat until the danger passed.

Chapter Thirty-Nine

"It all happened so fast," Eva would later recall. "It seemed as though no sooner than Captain LaRue had us close up our formation than the world exploded in a cacophony of noise, sound…I don't know which. But I do know it felt as though the cigarette boats were on us in no time with the high pitch of their turbo charged engines at the same time as not one but two helos out of Miami dropped out of nowhere. It would have been quite the show if it hadn't been so serious. We kept tight to the Tedi Bare, the fast boats did one loop around us and headed toward Ft. Lauderdale with the Coast Guard giving chase. The three captains were all busy on the radio as to what we should next. We did learn that the fast boats made it to the jetties before being intercepted. They had guns, actually had us out gunned but who were we to know, bales of marijuana and cocaine. The local police have them all in custody. After about an hour of us wondering what to do we decided to keep going and here we are. Now, Woody, I'll have another St. Pauli's Girl."

She pushed her empty toward the owner of the Red Lion. All three boats were now safely tucked into their respective slips in Bimini with the Mahalo staying at the Big Game Club. There would be the pre-tournament reception the following evening where Eva was getting a special recognition for her initiatives with the islands stray and homeless dogs, and then the competition would commence. It was to be a four-day tournament, with one day off at the discretion of each boat for a total of three fishing days.

Which day to take off was a science unto itself. Some captains wanted to get out of the gate fast in hopes they could set the bar high enough on day one that it would be difficult to catch them. Others, like Hank, wanted to listen in as to where the fish were, or more specifically where they weren't. This would give him an idea of where to head over the next three days. Either philosophy had its winners and losers. The final judge would be the weather forecast over the next four days.

After another meal of grilled wahoo along with island slaw and peas and rice, they all headed back to the Big Game Club saying their goodnights to Bones at the head of the dock.

"Although we are not going to fish in the tournament Thursday, I want everyone ready to push off by eight tomorrow. I want to get more practice with the kite and watch where the other boats are getting their action. Bones, be here by seven."

"No problem Cap. I will be here with ice and bait and will make up the regular lines until you teach me about the kite. Goodnight everyone."

As the other three strolled down the long dock to the Mahalo's berth, they passed not one but two guard stations. It was well known the chances Eva was taking by coming back to defend her title and the local police were going to do their best to protect her and the rest of the crew.

Once she stepped back onto the Mahalo, a sense of being at home rushed over her. The familiar smells and sights along with the gentle rocking of this magnificent fishing machine gave her a great deal of comfort. So many good memories had already been forged here and she was determined many more were yet to come.

Chapter Forty

Was it the coffee? It had to be the smell of coffee and not the sounds of several voices which had awakened her. She looked at her watch…Six-thirty. "My God what were they doing?" She looked over to the bed spot Calhoun usually occupied only to find it deserted as well. "Seems I'm the last to the party," she thought. "I'm sure Hank will have something to say about that so I might as well take my time since I'm already in trouble."

She emerged from her cabin ten minutes later only to be spotted by Hank. "Eva, grab that number two rod and get it outside and put it in its regular spot" and with that he was gone, back to the flying bridge where he started both engines. "Boy, he really is serious, not even a quip about my whereabouts."

She grabbed the rod as instructed, slid the salon doors open and was met with the sounds of organized confusion. She took a moment and had to make a conscience effort not to drop her jaw. Every marina was a hive of activity, that is, for the boats which still remained. Most had departed to go flex their fishing muscles somewhere off Bimini. Bones was busy making up baits and Calhoun was in his customary seat with his customary pipe full of Prince Albert smoking away. He gave her a quick glance, his blue eyes twinkling in excitement and anticipation. His dimpled smile let her know everything was going to be okay. In that one moment, she realized she fell in love with him all over again; an occurrence which seemed to happen with more regularity which she found difficult to explain. No words had to be exchanged…they both just knew.

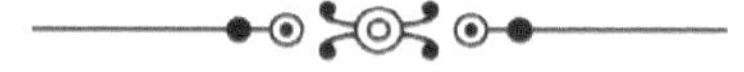

Chapter Forty-One

It was a perfect day for fishing. The blue sky was punctuated with white cotton candy cloud wisps. Seas were running two to three feet and the humidity had taken the day off.

Hank headed south, away from prying eyes so he could perfect his kite fishing technique. His intention was to swing back to the north later in the day, where most of the fleet was fighting it out. He didn't need a lot of fish, just two or three to get the feel for what they would be doing and to get everyone on the same page. Bones popped in a cassette tape of a new and upcoming artist by the name of Jimmy Buffett, a radical departure from the Rat Pack Calhoun so enjoyed. It immediately prompted a gruff question of what is that noise?

"Why Mr. Hipp, that's Jimmy Buffett! All the fishes in the ocean know Jimmy Buffett songs."

"Harumph!" came the one-word response.

With the island sounds of Buffett playing in the background, Hank went about the business of teaching Bones the nuances of kite fishing.

Being an old salt, it did not take long for him to catch on nor did it take long for the crew of the Mahalo to see results. Almost immediately, a wahoo crashed the lively bait followed in succession by a king mackerel, two small dolphin and a barracuda. Hank was pleased with the activity but realized the turnaround on getting a fish in the boat and the line redeployed was taking too long. They needed to be quicker.

They had been trolling for about fifteen minutes with all lines in save for the kite line when the water behind the bouncing bait lit up…a sail was making a run at the ballyhoo on the line. Before Hank could yell out "Five!" the predator had crashed the bait and was solidly hooked. Hank immediately grabbed the rod from its flying bridge holder, passed it to Bones who was standing below and nimbly placed it in the gimbal of the fighting chair where Eva awaited. The whole process took less than thirty seconds and was as seamless as Hank could hope. The team was ready and they knew it especially when Eva had little trouble reeling in and releasing the seventy-five-pound fish. There would be no celebratory flags flying when they returned. Hank saw no reason to give away their secret weapon any sooner than required.

Chapter Forty-Two

Such was not the case with their perceived main competitor. As they rounded the jetties into the harbor, they could hear the celebration coming from Brown's Dock where Captain Smickems, along with other tournament boats, was tied up. The music could not drown out the lyrics of "Take me home with you" or any Elvis song. LaRue was in his element, the few women around were screaming and his boat was adorned with flags depicting two sailfish caught and released. On the dock Hank could see half a dozen dolphin. All in all, a great days catch and had the tournament been in effect, The Tedi Bare would no doubt have a sizable lead.

As the Mahalo passed Brown's dock on their way to the Big Game Club, LaRue turned and glared at Hank who returned the silent challenge with a smile and a salute…all of it meant to get under the opposing captain's skin as none of it was a goodwill gesture. The posturing was on!

After the Mahalo got back to their dock and the crew washed it down, Hank called for a quick meeting. "First of all, I'm proud of how fast we got the knack of things with our kite. I believe it could be our difference maker. Let's remember, every rod that goes down goes to Eva. If she is tied up fighting a fish then Mr. Hipp takes it. No exceptions. This means Eva you have to be available from the time we get our first line wet until the last leader is in the boat. Now, what's really on my mind is Slayder. Things seem too normal..."

"Yeah, too normal to my way of thinking," chimed in Bones who got a withering stare from Hank for the interruption.

"Anyway, as I was saying, things seem to be too normal or too quiet for my comfort. Let's all keep our wits about us tonight at the pretournament dinner and awards. He's out there somewhere and we know he will show up...just when and where we don't know yet but at least we are better armed than the last time, if it comes to that. Questions?"

Hank felt like he was preaching to the choir but he also felt better about addressing the elephant in the room.

"OK, let's all get showered and Bones get back here in an hour and we will go collect some well-deserved hardware on behalf of Ms. Eva here.

Chapter Forty-Three

The celebration at the Calypso Club was far removed from the event they had attended a year ago when they celebrated Eva winning the female angler award. There was no island band and certainly no Princess Tanika. There was an open bar and plenty of food. The purpose of this meeting was to kick off the tournament, go over the rules as well as the point system assigned to various fish and to make sure everyone monitored the tournament radio frequency. Since most of the assembled group were veteran tournament participants, there were few questions of consequence. A reminder that it was a four-day event but fishing was allowed only over three days which was at the discretion of the captain.

Then the moment came when the Governor came forward to welcome all and describe the EVA (Every Vessel Assists) Awards for the work Eva had done in taking care of the stray animals on Bimini. He announced the program would be replicated on many of the other islands in the very near future. With that he called Eva to the front to accept a painting created by a local artist as the tribute for all of her work.

Eva began. "It is an honor to be recognized for what for me was a labor of love. I saw a need and tried to fix things as best I could. I think the way your community has embraced the coconut bowl challenge, especially by incorporating local art was not only brilliant bur ensured the success we have enjoyed. Hundreds of animals have been saved with better care all of it due to your concern.

I would also like to thank…."

She stopped in mid-sentence and stared at the back of the room in shock and horror for leaning up against the back wall, with arms crossed and a smirk she was way too familiar with, stood Slayder.

$$\bullet\circ\ \raisebox{0pt}{\Large\diamond\odot\diamond}\ \circ\bullet$$

Chapter Forty-Four

Catatonic. That was the only word which came to mind as Calhoun watched Eva freeze in mid -sentence. She was staring at someone or something in the back of the room. Then it hit him…Slayder! Calhoun spun around in his chair only to catch a glimpse of a figure hurriedly leaving the club. Without a word he reached back, grabbed Hank by the shoulder and yanked him to his feet. Bones was startled by whatever was going on but he jumped up in response to his boss's sudden urge to move.

Calhoun uttered two words which answered all the questions the crew of the Mahalo had and which served to put them into a higher gear. "It's him!"

The three of them tore out of the room reaching the door Slayder had just exited mere moments after he had gone. But the street was empty. It was as though Slayder had vanished just as he had before. The arrival of one of the islands most wanted had not gone unnoticed totally. Captain Shumate had been sitting in the back row dressed in civilian clothes as he was off duty and present more to honor Eva than to protect her. When Eva had frozen mid speech and he realized who was standing just a few feet from him, he too raced out from a side door in case Slayder attempted to run around the back of the building. He now came racing up to the crew of the Mahalo as they stood looking befuddled as to the whereabouts of their adversary. Moments later Eva came out after making apologies for her obvious distraction.

"Eva, this is enough!" sounded off a clearly distraught Calhoun. "Clearly, we can no longer keep putting your life in danger. We need to go home."

"To what?" Eva fired back. "Calhoun this has to end at some point or we will never be free of him." Gently cradling either side of his face, Eva looked deeply into his eyes. "I love you for so many reasons and it's for those reasons we draw the line here. I will no longer allow him to rule our lives by rumor and the fear it brings with it. We stop it now." And then with a gleam in her green eyes she summed up her decision. "Besides, I have a tournament to go win!"

Part Three

Chapter Forty- Five
Day One of the Bimini Big Game Rodeo Fishing Tournament

Eva was awakened by 5:30 the next morning with the now familiar aroma of fresh brewing coffee. Calhoun was, predictably, out of the bed and nowhere to be seen. Rubbing her sleep laden eyes, she took a moment to splash cold water on her face and to quickly brush her teeth. When she stepped outside her cabin, she was surprised to see the salon in a beehive of activity...well at least as much as three men could make it bumping into each other as they quickly removed rods from their ceiling mounted holders and placed them in the rod holders in the cockpit. She felt it best to stay out of the way for the moment so she quickly grabbed a cup of coffee from the galley and weaved her way to the fighting chairs outside. It wasn't long before Calhoun joined her.

"I thought we weren't fishing today so why all the frantic rushing around?"

"Hank wants to make this off day as much of a dress rehearsal as possible so we will start the tournament with those boats actually fishing and then go do our own thing." Calhoun barely looked up while he explained the plan as he was busy packing his pipe bowl with the mornings first load of tobacco. "The LeMans start is set for 8 a.m. sharp so we need to be on station prior to that."

At that moment Bones came out from the salon and made his way over to the iced bait where he began making those up for the days fishing by attaching colorful lures along with the bait of ballyhoo to the leader wire so they were ready to clip to the fishing line.

"And Hank?" queried Eva.

"He's in the engine room checking all his fluid levels before we crank up. Once we get underway it will get too hot down there to stay for any length of time" came Bones response.

Satisfied, Eva took a moment to look out at the dock where the same frantic activity was being replicated. She stood up and went all the way to the stern where she could catch a glimpse of Brown's dock and was not surprised to see it just as active. All she could think of was how much this looked like a fleet getting ready to sail to face some unknown adversary. It excited her and scared her at the same time. Could she hold up her end of the bargain and repeat as the winning female angler? Even more important, could the Mahalo win the whole thing?

She did not have long to contemplate the swirling questions as Hank now appeared and as serious as she had ever seen him.

"We have a lot of boats we are up against. This will not be easy so let's all relax and have fun and let the fish fall where they may. Bones, get up front and release the bow line. I'll grab the two spring lines on my way to the bridge. Calhoun, keep the stern line until the end and release it on my command."

Everyone performed as instructed so that within minutes they were free from the dock and headed to the jetties as other boats from other docks streamed out and joined them.

"Well, at least we have one thing on this boat no other boat in the tournament has" Eva said leaning into Calhoun so no one else could hear.

"What's that?"

"Hank!"

Chapter Forty-Six

The day was as beautiful as forecast. In fact, the entire weekend was predicted to have similar weather. Eva had made her way topside to enjoy the spectacle laid out before her. In the distance sat the tournament boat, festooned with seemingly dozens of colorful nautical flags. She was impossible to miss which was by design. No one was to pass her before the blare of its airhorn at 8 a.m. sharp signaling the start of the days fishing. From that moment, it was a race for each boat to get to its favorite fishing area before everyone else. This was one of Hank's tests for the morning. How fast could the Mahalo go so he would know for tomorrow's start. From the looks of all the boats, it was hard for Eva to believe anyone opted out from this first day but Hank had assured her some twenty boats had passed on this day's fishing.

It took another five minutes before Hank approached the invisible line no boat was to cross. He threw the Mahalo into reverse for a moment in order to stop its forward momentum then put the boat in neutral where it slowly rocked with the gentle swells of a flat sea.

"Five Minutes!" came the disemboweled voice from the tournament boat over the radio. Eva looked both left and right soaking in the magnificent scene of dozens of boats floating in a line ready to go win a tournament where every fish counted, regardless of type.

"Sixty Seconds, thirty, ten, nine" the countdown continued until the ear-splitting sound of the airhorn could be heard through the air as well as over the radio. The stillness of the day erupted into an explosion of engine noises as every boat went full throttle simultaneously. Hank was focused on how well the Mahalo responded and was not disappointed to see her in the front quarter of the pack and putting distance between her and the rest of the boats. Now he knew what to expect so it came as a surprise when he heeled over hard to port and put the Mahalo on a westerly course while the balance of the tournament boats continued north and east toward the usually fertile fishing grounds of the Bimini Shelf and the Gulf Stream.

Chapter Forty-Seven

They ran for forty-five minutes before Hank deemed them far enough away to risk bringing out the kite line. This area was not normally as good for fishing but today's point was to practice more so than to catch fish.

As was his custom, Hank monitored the radio channel where most of the captains did their reporting. It seemed the Saga was having a good day with quite a run on dolphin. Suddenly the report was interrupted by a giant sneeze followed by three more. It was so loud even Eva could hear it from the cockpit below where she waited patiently to catch her first fish of the day even though it would not count.

"Hank, what is that noise? Is someone sneezing into the radio?"

"Unfortunately, I recognize that sound and it is not someone but something. Welcome to the sound Louise makes when they are in the fish. Obviously LaRue wants everyone to know he is deep into the hunt, especially since the Saga has a hot hand right now.

Alright, I'm deploying the kite. Heads up everyone."

As expected, the kite immediately began its wind dance once it was released. The temptation to just watch it perform often led to admonishment from Hank as he reminded everyone they were here to catch fish, not watch a kite, so keep their eyes on the wake.

An hour into the kite's deployment there had still been no action, on any line, so it startled Eva when Hank screamed out "Five!" … the kite line.

As so often rehearsed, Hank handed the rod to Bones who put it into the gimble in Eva's chair while removing the rod which had been occupying space in the chairs' rod holder.

The rod instantly bent over as the line screamed off the reel. Whatever had decided to dance with the kite's bait was big. All Eva could do was hold onto the rod with both hands and wait until this fish wore down. Ten minutes later, her patience paid off as the line stopped being stripped from the rod, allowing Eva to slowly begin the task of bringing in her mystery fish.

Almost an hour after the initial hookup her patience was rewarded as Bones leaned over the stern with the larger gaff and with two attempts finally brought in a huge bull dolphin. The fish had spent itself in the fight and once bought on board and placed in the fishbox it was not heard from again.

"Good job everyone!" praised Hank. "I think we are ready to begin our three days of fishing. Since we know there are few fish in this area, I suggest we bring the lines in and start back. The tournament boat will sound its airhorn at 4 p.m. ending the days tournament except those who may be hooked up. It's up to those captains to report in if that is the case. And just so you know, Captain Larue has the most exotic fish reported caught today, a blue marlin. Saga reports fifteen dolphin boated which may make her the leader in point totals after day one."

Chapter Forty-Eight

As they rounded the jetties heading back toward their slip, Hank noticed a commotion at the weigh in dock at Brown's Marina. Due to the number of boats fishing this tournament, there were two weigh in docks, the other being at the Big Game Club. Hank could not tell what was going on, only that it seemed to involve the Saga as she was still tied up, taking up space from any other boat that might want to have their days catch properly registered. Hank decided they would all walk up from their berth at the Big Game Club to investigate the disturbance before they washed the Mahalo down.

It took only a minute from the time they arrived at Brown's dock before they were shocked with the cause. The Saga had been accused of cheating, that several, if not all, of her catch were frozen indicating they had been caught days earlier and attempted to pass off as todays efforts. The owner was furious, the captain looked as though he was about to have a stroke and the only other angler just stood by, totally unsure as to what he should do.

But the evidence was indisputable. Having summoned the vet who happened to be on the island that weekend as part of the EVA project and the only medical professional around, the determination was made. Upon gutting the fish, ice crystals were discovered indicating these fish had been frozen for at least several days. The actions the tournament committee took were swift and final. The Saga was disqualified, required to return back to her homeport immediately and banned from any Bahamas tournament for a minimum of two years, this last edict being appealable at a later date. For now, they were to leave and suddenly LaRue's boat held first position after day one with a total catch of one blue marlin, two barracuda and a (legit) dolphin. Daddy's Girl was second and The Perfect Season was third. The Mahalo would start her tournament in the morning, secret weapon and all.

Chapter Forty-Nine
Day Two of the Tournament

Five Thirty that morning found everyone up and prepping the boat. However, they were hit with disappointing news. Somehow a cold front had materialized leaving enough of a steady drizzle that foul weather gear would be required. And Hank was taking it the hardest.

"This weather is just damp enough to soak the kite." He reported. "That will make the cloth too heavy to fly today so now we will have to use our skills without our secret weapon. Miami weather says this front should be out of here by early afternoon but I don't want to expose our secret for only a half day of fishing. Once the other boats see what we are doing you can bet your house on the fact they will have similar rigs flown over immediately on Chalks or brought over by some friend.

"Now be careful on the cockpit deck," he continued. "This type of drizzle will make every surface slicker than we are used to so stay aware.

This weather will also knock the seas down a bit. Not ideal but we are all dealing with the same conditions. From what I can gather, most of the action yesterday was just north of us so we will initially head in that direction."

"By the way, Eva, good job on your fish yesterday. Coming in at forty-three pounds would have you fourth female in the tournament but we weren't official so all I can say is we know we can do it so let's bust our tails for the next three days and not worry about anything else. Focus, people, on the task at hand and the rest will take care of itself! Now let's cast off."

Hank was a good Catholic and his Knute Rockne speech would have fit perfectly in Notre Dame lore. In fact, Eva found herself almost saluting at the end of it. The Gipper wasn't on board but his spirit sure was!

They repeated the actions from the day before, letting the lines go and freeing the boat as it joined the convoy of other vessels making their way to the tournament boat. The talk from the night before centered around the Saga and what possible reason would they have to cheat. No one understood but it cast a shadow over the entire tournament enveloping them all in a gloom only matched by the weather.

As they made their way out of the jetties, Eva gingerly climbed the ladder to the flying bridge to get a better view of the surrounding boats and to gain a bit of shelter from the steady drizzle which seemed to find its way into areas the foul weather suit did not cover. She hoped for an active day so her concentration would center on her fishing rather than her misery.

"Hank, my dolphin may not have won anything yesterday but it sure was good the way you fried up chunks to mix with our peas and rice for dinner last night. I swear, if you ever decide to give up the sea, you need to open a restaurant here on Bimini and I will be your head waitress and barkeeper!"

"Always good to have a fallback" came the terse reply as Hank was all business with little time for idle talk. Realizing that, and the starting horn having sounded, Eva slid further into the flying bridge cushion area which protected her from the driving drizzle as they raced to whatever location Hank had in mind.

The sea remained flat as the Mahalo surged ahead of most of the competing boats. Hank's head was once again on a swivel, not only checking where he was in relation to the other participants, but also to discern who might be his chief competition beyond those boaters who currently held the lead.

"Eva, grab the wheel and keep us on our present heading. Actually, the auto-pilot will do that, just make sure we don't run over anyone. I'm going below to grab the more powerful binoculars."

Before she could respond he was down the ladder. She heard the salon doors close so she knew he had headed below but before she could actually reflect upon his sudden disappearance, he was back with a larger set of binoculars in hand. He trained them on a boat that was running several hundred yards off his port bow.

"Crap!"

"What's wrong Hank?" she queried totally unsure as to what could have caused such a sudden and visceral reaction.

"I thought I recognized that boat. She's the Gypsea. They will be a tough out, may be even our chief competition."

"Do you know the captain? Have you fished against him before?" Eva was getting ready to pepper Hank with a dozen questions before he held up his hand signaling her to stop.

"The thing about the Gypsea is she has no permanent captain. The owner rotates the best he can get at any point in time. No, the thing that makes her such a challenge is the owner himself. Probably one of the best if not the best angler in the world. He just needs a captain to drive his boat. He has a great instinct as to where the fish are. Things just got a good bit more interesting."

Chapter Fifty

Hank continued running at full throttle for another ten minutes when he suddenly pulled the throttles back to a trolling speed.

"Bones, get lines one and three in the water now! Eva, get below and get in your chair!" The puzzled look on Eva's face was matched by the occupants of the other boats as they passed, continuing the race toward the Bimini Shelf and the Gulfstream.

Bones had barely spooled out line three when the rod suddenly bent over. This line was in Calhoun's chair so immediately he got up and surrendered it to his paramour and current female champion angler.

Eva jumped in and took the rod from Bones. As she started to reel, she realized she either had a fish which was racing toward the boat or, in more likelihood, a very small catch.

As she reeled, she looked up at Hank who was standing at the railing of the flying bridge and gave him a quizzical look.

"Just reel" came his response and no sooner had he said it than Bones reached over the side, grabbed the leader wire and pulled in a seven-pound bonito.

Now Eva was really confused. How did he know to suddenly stop here? However, before she could ask Hank was once again barking instructions. "Bones, get that fish in the live well and secure the other rods. With that, Hank pushed the Mahalo back to full throttle and resumed, what was now a chase, to the Gulfstream.

The bonito barely fit into the live well whose purpose was just as the name implied…to keep fish, usually bait, alive. This box was located mid deck between the two fighting chairs. A series of holes in the bottom allowed fresh seawater to filter through while keeping the water level even with the waterline of the boat.

Eva headed back up to the bridge, still fighting the dampness which permeated everything as the drizzle had now become a fine mist obscuring any visual beyond one hundred yards or so. This would get to be dicey the closer they got to the fishing grounds as no one wanted to run up on another boat or get tangled in their lines. The sound of foghorns notified others where a particular boat may be.

"Okay, how did you know to stop right there captain?" came the question which had consumed her from the start.

"I saw, what appeared to be the confluence of two bodies of water but I knew that couldn't be so I figured it may be fish being chased just beneath the surface and it was. Now, I have plans for that fish is why I'm keeping him alive. You'll see as soon as the weather clears up. Now no more questions, return to your seat and get ready for whatever may come at us next!"

Knowing better than to argue, Eva silently retreated back to her fishing chair in the cockpit below.

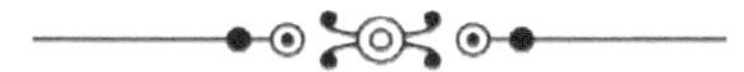

Chapter Fifty- One

What came at them next was the last thing they expected…sneezing sounds coming over the radio on the tournament frequency. It was so loud it even caused Eva to stand up and look around.

"That, folks, is the infernal sound of Captain LaRue's pet animal, Louise. He is letting everyone know that he is either in the fish or hopes to soon be." Before Hank could get any further worked up, he yelled, "Two! Three!" Both lines went down within scant seconds of one another causing both anglers to grab their rods and begin reeling.

"Barracuda on both. Normally I would be mad about those scavengers hitting my baits but today they count for points. Let's get 'em in!"

Before ten minutes had lapsed, Bones had boated both fish and had them secure in the fishbox. Just as Bones finished getting the lines back out, Mother Nature stepped in. The mist began to lift and a bright orb, set directly above them, started to melt away the balance of the moisture which had tormented them all morning.

"The sun! Finally!" yelped a delighted Eva as she peeled off her foul weather gear revealing her fishing attire of bikini and skimpy top. It was actually a yellow polka dotted outfit made famous years ago in song. She started to take her top off as well since it was her custom but thought better of it and left it in place. "Now I feel human!" she declared.

With the arrival of the sun at midday, the temperatures climbed and the fish sounded…heading toward cooler waters. The only thing worse than no activity was listening to the incessant sneezing of Louise accompanied by some off key Elvis song courtesy of LaRue. Yes, they were in the fish, a school of small dolphin. They were scoring points while everyone suffered through the cacophony of noise assailing everyone in the fleet.

"Make it stop, Hank! Please!" came Eva's plea which was shared by everyone but no one could do a thing. And to make matters worse, the fleet, as a whole, did not catch another thing the balance of the day. LaRue was first with six dolphin and amazingly enough, the Mahalo was second with one barely alive bonito and two thirty-five-pound barracuda. The billfish had been out there as reported by several boats…they just weren't biting. Amazingly, Gypsea was skunked with so many others… an occurrence that had seldom been witnessed.

Chapter Fifty-Two

As they came back through the jetties and passed along Brown's dock, Hank could not help but observe two island policemen ahead, waiting on the docks of The Big Game Club. He was filled with a sense of dread as their presence seldom carried with it good news.

As they came alongside their berth, both uniformed police assisted by catching the lines thrown by Bones and Calhoun. Eva had earlier gone below and thus was not yet aware of the police. She came out of the salon at the same time Hank killed the engines. She took one look at their welcoming committee and groaned, "Oh no."

Lost in the group was Captain Shumate as he was still in plain clothes much as he was on the evening Slayder had appeared at the kickoff dinner.

"Permission to come aboard?" Calhoun waved him on and once they were settled in the salon, Shumate got right to the point.

"Last night we had a half dozen bales of marijuana, better known as square groupers, wash up on the north end. We surmise your friend Slayder is back at it. Instead of confiscating them, we left them where they were but we hid a tracking device in two of the bales. We are hopeful those will be recovered and returned to Slayder and with any luck we will be able to catch him. The reason I am here is to not only inform you of our plans but to let you know we are going to keep uniformed officers around you pretty much anytime you are on the island and not fishing. This is for everyone's protection, but especially for Eva's. This is not a suggestion but is by the decree of the Governor himself so you really have no choice in the matter. Go about your routines and let us handle the rest."

"Oh, like you have done such a great job so far." Eva muttered under her breath.

Only Calhoun caught what she said but a quick shake of his head quieted her down.

"Thank you, Captain. We appreciate your concern and your protection. But if we are to go about our normal duties, we need to get you off the boat so we can wash it down and start rigging lines for tomorrow. However, before you go, where did the term square grouper come from?"

"It is the nickname given to ganja which is either thrown overboard or tossed from airplanes in order not to get caught with them when arrest appears to be imminent. I believe it is a term coined by your Coast Guard."

And with that, Shumate left with his two other officers standing guard on the dock.

"Since we are all here, I need to point something out about tomorrow." It was now Hank's turn to speak. "You may not realize it but the leading boats, with the exception of us, have to take tomorrow off as they have already fished two days. We will be the lead boat at the start tomorrow and I intend for us to break free of the pack. If we can do that and hold everyone off on Sunday…. well, you get the picture. There are a lot of fish to be caught between now and then so let's get this boat cleaned and prepped and dinner tonight will be on me!"

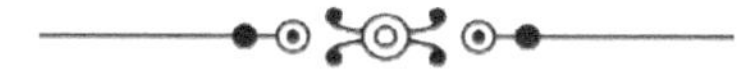

Chapter Fifty- Three
Day Three of the Tournament

Five thirty found everyone preparing for a day of fishing. Bones had just arrived with bags of ice and additional canned drinks giving a couple to the police who had watched over them all evening. Calhoun, along mostly with Eva's help, was preparing sandwiches for the day while Hank went into the now cooled engine room to check on his power plant and auxiliary pumps. Everyone knew that once they took their positions, it would be difficult to leave until the final horn sounded from the tournament boat. There was also a great deal of pride and exhilaration in the knowledge they were the lead boat and everyone would be chasing them.

At seven they pushed off from the dock joining the fishing armada heading to sea for this day's battle. As fate would have it, the Gypsea joined up alongside them, looking every bit as the main competition for the day and possibly the entire tournament. Everyone was now all business.

As they cleared the jetties, Hank was delighted to be met with a southerly breeze kicking the waves up to between two to three feet. There was not a cloud in the sky but the early morning sun belied the promise of a hot day. As far as Hank was concerned, it was close to ideal fishing weather. He suspected it would result in a large number of fish being boated. He would prove to be correct.

With the sound of the airhorn, the armada leapt into action. Every boat was full throttle heading toward the Gulfstream and/or the Bimini Shelf. Not so with Hank.

"Bones, get up here and take the wheel. I want you to head toward that Man 'O War circling out off our port bow. I'm going below to get our bonito ready".

As soon as Bones made it up to the bridge, Hank slid down the handrails landing him squarely in the middle of the cockpit where both Calhoun and Eva dutifully waited. He went to the bait well and pulled out the struggling fish. Using two pair of treble hooks, he was able to surgically place the hooks without killing the fish, leaving plenty of life and action in the bait. With that chore accomplished, he returned to the bridge with the fish in hand. Pulling the kite out of the bridge locker, he attached a leader to the bait and to rod number five. With a mighty heave, and allowing the bait to spool free, he tossed it all over the side where the kite immediately caught the breeze and started jigging on its own. Hank had barely enough time to finish getting the line out on rod number five when he froze. One heartbeat, two and then on three he screamed "FIVE!" As loud as he ever had. Bones raced down the steps to the cockpit, took the rod from Hank and had just given it to Eva when their quarry hit.

Coming clean out of the water, shaking its bill from side to side and almost tail dancing on the water's surface was a white marlin. Not rare but unusual and surely worth extra points. Since no other lines had yet to be put out, the show was totally Eva's and what a show it turned out to be. The marlin, now fully hooked by the treble hooks came roaring out of the water again but Eva reeled hard, keeping the line tight. Other boats, passing by and giving a wide clearance out of courtesy, reported the Mahalo was hooked up. Hank got on the radio and confirmed. the Mahalo was in a fight before most boats had even gotten their lines wet.

Forty-five minutes were rapidly turning toward an hour when the marlin suddenly stopped. It had been a battle of strength and determination but Eva had finally worn down her opponent. She reeled hard to get the fish close enough for Bones, using the larger gaff, could hook the fish and haul it in. A couple of strikes with the Billy club and it was all over. Eva had the first bill for a female angler in the tournament, which ultimately weighed in at just over eighty pounds. The sweat poured off of her in tiny rivers so she welcomed the bucket of seawater Bones poured over her to help cool her down. She looked up and smiled at Calhoun, with her dimples flashing to show just how happy she was. Her expression moved Calhoun to get out of his chair, go over to hug and congratulate her and tell her how proud he was. He was just starting to tell her how much he loved her when a booming voice came from above.

"What's all the lollygagging about? Get that blood from the fish off my deck and let's get some lines out. Did all of you forget we have a tournament to win? Jeez!"

Hank turned back to the captain's chair mainly so those below would not see the giant grin etched across his face. The Gypsea may have a world class angler on board but he would not trade his crew for anyone.

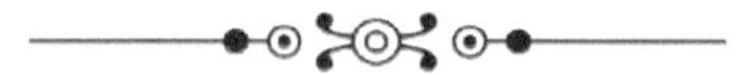

Chapter Fifty-Four

It was then the screaming started. Dozens of boats cussing, complaining and overall accusing the Mahalo of just plain cheating. It was all about the kite. The tournament boat was so overwhelmed by complaints that they took the unusual step of initiating the emergency call signal giving two quick short blasts of the airhorn. This was the prearranged sign for all captains to get on the tournament frequency immediately.

After five minutes, the tournament chair made the announcement the Mahalo had done nothing wrong by deploying a kite. In fact, the boats were informed Captain Hank, after not seeing anything in the rules book had reached out and expressly inquired as to its legality, an avenue any one of the other boats could have used. This was the only admonishment the tournament director had, followed by a quick reminder that if the complaining continued, that boat and crew would be disqualified from the tournament. The threat had the desired result as no more complaining was heard and the fishing continued. Hank knew he did not make many friends on the day but after all, they had a prize to win and would use any legal means at their disposal to do so.

Hank headed toward the Man 'O War he had been watching as the bird seemed very interested in something below the broken weed line about five hundred yards off the starboard bow. He slowed his speed, giving time for Bones to get all lines in the water and to especially get the kite baited and handed up to the bridge where Hank attached it to the outrigger and carefully tossed it over the side, allowing for the speed of the boat and the prevailing breeze to take over pushing the kite about fifty feet above the trailing wake.

Again, it took less than five minutes before Hank sung out "FIVE!" as a pretty good-sized dolphin crashed the bait. Now, there was especially no doubt in Hanks mind that the kite held a special allure to anything swimming in the vicinity. Once again, Hank handed the rod to Bones who gave it to Eva to begin reeling in. In the meantime, Hank yelled out "ONE!" then "THREE!". Calhoun grabbed the first line while Bones spooled out line three in order to get it away from the action so no lines became tangled and with the hopes that what was believed to be a school of dolphin, would stay with the boat.

For their efforts, they managed to bring in a total of four dolphin with Eva's being the largest, a thirty-two-pound bull dolphin. It, too, would help her overall in the female scoring classification although her boated marlin continued to lead all female anglers at the time.

As things began to slow down as a result of the midday sun, Hank had a chance to listen into the tournament radio where he learned the Gypsea was hooked into two sails at the same time. With only one angler, it would take time to get one boated before attempting to bring the other sail in. Hank had no doubt the angler on board could do it and as time would prove, he did boat both sails, a rare accomplishment and a testimony to his skills.

Chapter Fifty-Five

As the day began to ebb, several billfish were caught among the tournament boats. Eva managed a nice size king mackerel who, in her opinion, looked like a strong first cousin to a barracuda. The remaining lines were barren, no fish seemed to be interested.

Then an interesting phenomenon began to take place. Starting in late afternoon, a small squadron of private planes of various makes and models began arriving at the airstrip in South Bimini.

"What do you make of all those planes suddenly showing up, Hank?" quired the ever-curious Eva.

"I am not quite sure but I have a pretty good idea but before I get everyone on edge, let's see what tomorrow brings."

"Now that's as mysterious a response as there ever has been from you. You have my interest but I know better than to push. So…how much longer do we have today?"

Hank took note of the position of the sun, the placement of the tournament fleet and where the Mahalo was in relationship to the fleet…weighing his options as to whether to continue. He also stole a glance at his watch which revealed he only had forty-five minutes of fishing time left anyway.

"Let's bring 'em in. I think we are done for the day. We can go ahead and get these fish weighed ahead of everyone else. Besides, as near as I can figure, Eva still has a nice lead and while I would like to pull off a double by winning the overall tournament as well, I think we may be just outside the winner's circle sitting around sixth overall as best as I can figure. But you never know. We are due for a full moon tonight and with the right current we could find some fish tomorrow looking for food. Did you guys notice how the ocean was green on one side of the current and deep blue on the other? That's where we want to be, dead center of the confluence of those two currents. And…" The last bit of his talk was drowned out by another private plane on final approach.

"What the hell?" Eva pondered as she watched the plane disappear from view.

Forty-five minutes later they pulled up to the weigh-in station at Brown's Marina. Eva's bull dolphin ended up being the largest caught overall on the day and her mackerel was the largest boated buy a female angler. She sat comfortably in the lead but knowing Hank, she would not be allowed to enjoy her lead until the final day was over.

As they departed the weigh in station in order to make room for the next boat, they all looked to the Big Game Club and as feared or either true to form, sat four policemen in uniform as well as Captain Shumate.

"Looks like we have another welcoming committee" observed Hank.

"Yeah, and I am about over them dogging our every step…Slayder or no Slayder!" came the exasperated response from Eva.

With plenty of help on the dock in the form of Her Majesty's Police, it took no time for the Mahalo to get tied off and the shore power plugged in.

"I guess this is the part where I ask you on board?" offered a surly Calhoun who had picked up on Eva's mood as he directed his question to Captain Shumate.

"No need" came the polite reply. "I can stand here to deliver what I believe is good news…we have found Slayder!"

It was not uncommon for people to stroll the docks looking at what each boat had captured on that day of fishing. Thus the gasp that sprang from Eva was loud enough to draw the attention of others, even those working on the dock.

"We have not arrested him…yet! We have him under surveillance. Now I know you are going to ask why we have not moved on him and the answer is simple. We have it on good authority that he is going to attempt to smuggle out a large quantity of marijuana and cocaine sometime within the next day or two. We believe he will try to blend in with all of the private planes leaving after the tournament and take advantage of the confusion surrounding so many close departures. We want to grab him with the contraband on board his plane so we know we have an air tight case against him with evidence in hand.

I know our track record has not been the best, but we have over fifty officers watching him and the area as we have flown over our own special forces group to join in the arrest. There is, quite literally, nowhere he can go without our knowing. The next move is his."

Even though her tone of voice had softened considerably, Eva could not restrain herself from having the last word. "I'll believe it when I see it."

"Indeed, you shall madam. Indeed, you shall." With a sharp turn reminiscent of a military about-face, Captain Shumate departed leaving the four other officers to stand watch over the Mahalo and her crew as they prepared for the final day of the tournament and whatever may follow after.

Chapter Fifty-Six
Final Day of the Tournament

R outine. Everyone had settled into it as the boat was prepared for this final and crucial day. Bones had brought ice and drinks on board, Hank was in the now cooled engine room running his checks while Calhoun and Eva brought out the rods they would use, placing them in various holders and then crowded one another in the galley making sandwiches which would be grabbed on the fly, activity permitting. No words were spoken which underscored the seriousness of the entire crew. Banter had no place on the Mahalo this day.

At a little after seven, all lines were cast off, waves were given to the four policemen who had stood guard throughout the night and the Mahalo joined the steady stream of boats heading toward the tournament boat waiting one thousand yards from the jetties. As if on cue, The Gypsea joined in, pulling away from Browns Dock and running parallel with Captain

Hank who had gathered his crew on the flying bridge.

"There is no need for a pep talk from me today. We are going to go out and do our best to win a tournament. I checked the leaderboard this morning and while Eva has the lead right now among female anglers, I will take nothing for granted so our first priority is to feed her as many lines as we can. Unless otherwise engaged, every strike needs to be handed off to her. As a team we are currently fifth. I'm not going to lie to you, trying to leapfrog four other boats to win this thing is difficult. It is not impossible, so keep that in mind. Every fish counts for something so let's get as many somethings as we can! Understood?"

"Yes Sir!" Bones replied as he headed back to the fishing cockpit below.

Eva responded with a mock salute and then to everyone's surprise a quick kiss on the cheek to Hank. "For luck" she explained as she, too, disappeared below. Calhoun continued to sit on the bench surrounding the console, taking out his pipe and reloading it before lighting it up. "May be my last chance today so I thought I would stay up here and enjoy a last smoke." He took in the scene unfolding around him…dozens of boats spilling out of the jetties all headed toward the tournament boat which was still festooned with various colored flags and pennants.

The sun itself added to the palate of colors as it changed from red to orange, on its way to a bright yellow. The early morning chill was quickly dissipating

"Boss, I need you to get below as well. In about ten minutes we will all get the starting horn and once that happens its full speed. I need you to assist Bones with the live mullet we have for the kite as I am curious to see if my theory on why so many private planes flew in yesterday is accurate."

"It's your boat captain. Let's make the most of it." And with that said, Calhoun joined the others below.

Once Calhoun took his place in his fighting chair, he looked over toward Eva who was shivering in spite of wearing a light windbreaker over her bikini.

"You okay?"

"Never better. Mostly nerves and excitement. I'm not cold if that is what you mean. Heck, I'm so wrapped up in this warm tropical air it gives me a sense of comfort kinda like being underneath my favorite childhood blanket." She saw the quizzical look fleetingly cross Calhoun's face. "I don't know how to explain it, I have never been so content and it feels…delicious!" She reached out for his hand, took it and gave it a squeeze. "Thank you…for everything. I love you more than I can ever adequately express to you."

The moment was shattered as the tournament airhorn blared, and fifty plus boats went from idle to full speed. Bones leaned over to Calhoun and asked for his assistance in getting the kite ready to bait in order to deploy. The final day had begun.

Chapter Fifty-Seven

As soon as the Mahalo planed out and was able to hit maximum running speed, Hank took a slight turn to the west, looking for the area where the stream and the ocean met which should be teeming with opportunities. Bones managed to get a mullet from the live bait well and with Calhoun's help, set within it another treble hook combo since that had served them well in the past. Lines one through four were baited and the lines run up into the outriggers with the only thing remaining to do was throw the bait over the side and free spool to the area they wanted it in. As soon as Hank decided to slow to trolling speed, the Mahalo would have five baited lines in the water in less than a minute.

It was barely ten minutes later when Hank spotted the merging of ocean and Gulf Stream. He slowed the boat to trolling speed and barked at Bones to get the kite line deployed. Hank readied the kite and as soon as Bones told him he was ready, he tossed it over the side so the breeze would capture it and it would begin its dance trying to entice anything which may be lurking below. Bones immediately went to lines three and four and spooled them out while Calhoun did the same with lines one and two. Now came the hard part…waiting.

With no birds in sight nor any discernable weed line to follow, Hank elected to turn back toward the majority of the fleet. He had barely completed his turn when he heard the sound he dreaded most…Louise sneezing. Obviously LaRue, Captain of the Tedi Bare, was into fish somewhere but at this distance Hank could not tell which boat was his. Daddy's Girl radioed in that Tedi Bare was hooked up with a billfish and moments later LaRue radioed the tournament boat to confirm.

All the while Hank kept his head on his proverbial swivel, surveying the five lines he had out. "Three!" came the shout from the bridge. Eva's line. Bones raced over, snatching the rod from its holder and deftly placing it in the gimbal between her legs. "Reel!" he shouted although he needn't have wasted his breath as Eva was now an experienced angler and had her prey well hooked and headed toward the stern much against its will.

"Barracuda" reported Hank. Let's get that fish in and rebait that line. I'm going to make a slight turn to starboard so you guys can see what I have suspected all along."

As he began his turn, Eva managed to get the leader wire in allowing Bones to grab it and swing the fish into the fishbox where it tried to escape by flopping about.

"Oh my God!" exclaimed Calhoun. "Would you look at that?" Eva followed his gaze and was just as surprised. Before them was the majority of the tournament fleet and springing up from them were kites, like so many mushrooms after a spring rain.

"Just as I suspected" trumpeted a somewhat gloating Hank. "All those planes coming in yesterday were bringing their owners those kites after we had flown ours. They may think it levels the playing field but all of you know it's one thing to have a kite, it's another to know how to use it. That's why I had us practicing. I'll be curious to see just how successful those guys are who are using them for the first time."

"Eight, I count eight" reported Eva. She had no sooner reported the kite count when their own kite took a sudden deep dive releasing itself from the outrigger at the same time.

"Five!" Screamed Hank. "Billfish on five." Hank handed the rod down to Bones who gave it to Eva. Calhoun got busy bringing the other lines in to avoid tangling them up. "Well at least we know the kite can work!" smiled Calhoun as Eva began the task of fighting this newest adversary and as Hank radioed the tournament boat to report the Mahalo was hooked up. Best of all…. Louise had stopped her obnoxious sneezing.

Chapter Fifty-Eight

Hank had glanced at his watch, as he always did when a billfish was hooked. From the time he noted until the time Bones was reaching over the stern with gaff in hand had been less than forty-five minutes. Bones grabbed the leader wire and hauled the sailfish on board giving it a couple of whacks with the Billy club just to make sure it would cause no trouble. Eva was covered in a fine sheen of sweat, having long ago shed the windbreaker she had on. Her smile, dimples and all, was nothing short of contagious.

"We did it!" she exclaimed while smiling from ear to ear. Hank looked down from the bridge and noted the size of the just boated fish. He estimated it to be around forty-five pounds so in one of those inexplicable coincidences basically a pound boated for every minute fought.

"Let's get that kite back out!" he barked. "No time to pat ourselves on the back. And by the way, while you were fighting your fish Eva, the Tedi Bare lost their billfish. I heard it was a nice sized marlin. He may still be hungry so we will see if we have any luck with him. And oh, by the way, let me be the first to congratulate you. By my calculations you are the top female angler for this tournament once again. Unless one of the other six women gets into a school of billfish, I believe the one you just boated makes it hard to catch you on points".

Eva took a quick bow followed by a longer hug from Calhoun. Bones even gave her a squeeze around the shoulders. While not official, they had come to do what they had intended. To win the female angler and to assist in the capture of Slayder; assuming he was as bottled up as Captain Shumate claimed. Could they make this a trifecta and win the tournament as well? If Hank had anything to do with it.

"Let's Go! Get those lines in the water! There are fish to catch and a tournament to win!"

Chapter Fifty-Nine

Hank made a slow turn toward the area where the majority of the tournament boats were working. He instructed Bones to come topside while he went below to quickly grab one of the premade sandwiches, taking full advantage of what little downtime he had. With sandwich and soft drink in hand, he stepped back out onto the cockpit where both Calhoun and Eva were dutifully watching over their respective lines.

Hank sat on the fishbox with his back to the stern so he could see them both while he spoke. "I want to share something with you guys. Most of the boats are congregated in one area. No matter how big this ocean is, these folks tend to cluster where the action is. Sometimes, they do not pay attention to where they are in relationship to other boats and they may cross our stern unintentionally cutting our lines. Especially with these weekend warriors, not so much with professional captains. My point is we may have to suddenly start reeling very fast to avoid having our lines cut so be aware. Additionally, we have a dozen or so boats trying to figure out how to kite fish for the first time. We know the kite is unpredictable in where it goes, but they don't. I've already heard over the tournament channel of a couple of near misses as boats go chasing their kites rather than doing just the opposite. So, we are now a couple of hundred yards away from the edge of the fleet. I'm going to start a slow turn to port and begin a racetrack pattern as we have done so many times in the past"

"Any questions?"

Calhoun and Eva never got a chance to ask.

Chapter Sixty

"FIVE!" Screamed Bones. Hank turned to look behind him and had just enough time to see the kite come crashing down into the water. Whatever had just hit that bait had hit it with such suddenness and ferocity that the line never had a chance to snap out of the out rigger. He continued to watch as the kite folded up upon itself and then disappeared below the surface. It was only the zing of the line spooling out that brought him back to the moment.

"Bones, hand me that rod, be careful 'cause whatever we have back there is not fooling around. Did you see it?"

"No, boss. I was looking forward to make sure we did not get tangled with anyone even though we had a little space before we got to the other boats. Sorry."

"ZING!" The line was spooling out at an unusual rate of speed.

"Hand me the rod Bones. Quickly, before this thing takes all of our line."

Bones had to wrestle the rod out of its holder so great was the downward pressure on it. He managed to pass it below to Hank who was surprised by the weight on the other end. With a slight stumble, he managed to jab it into the gimbal of Eva's chair, where she waited with more than just a little nervous anticipation.

"Calhoun, clear the deck. Get all lines in, put the rods up in the salon so they are out of the way and then go below and get the big gaff. Grab some of the fishing gloves out of my tackle box in my cabin. I have a feeling Eva is going to need them."

Calhoun did not need to respond as all he needed to see was Eva and the rod both bent over nearly in half. All she could do was hold on. He would get those gloves as soon as possible as he feared she might begin to develop blisters on her hands given the force of whatever she was up against.

Hank raced up the ladder to the bridge, instructed Bones to get below to help Calhoun then called into the tournament boat that the Mahalo was hooked up but he had no idea as to what. Hank took the boat out of gear to reduce the drag and pressure on the line and not a moment too soon as Eva's arms began to quiver, a sign of early exhaustion.

With Bones to help, Calhoun quickly went below to grab the gaff and more importantly the fishing gloves. He left the gaff in the salon where it would stay out of the way and then he went to see how he could manage to help get the gloves on Eva without touching the rod and thus disqualifying this fish.

As if on cue, the outbound spooling stopped. Eva took advantage of this slight respite to take one hand off the rod while Calhoun placed a glove over the free hand then repeated the process. Within thirty seconds both hands were gloved giving her a greater grip and without risking any disqualification.

"Need anything?" he asked of his paramour.

"Water and see if Hank can turn this boat so the cockpit is in the shade. It's getting mighty hot out here."

Calhoun went to the bridge to deliver the requests from his top angler. As a result, Hank put one engine in gear to minimize drag and slowly turned the stern away from the sun.

"Eva, see if you can begin to reel in some of the line. I believe we may have worn out our fish just a bit so let's try to bring him closer".

Eva could only muster a nod of the head and then begin the process of bringing the rod up to her chin and reeling hard as she lowered it as far as it would go. The amount of weight she was attempting to boat was staggering…at least to her. Calhoun appeared with a gallon of water, gently holding it to her lips so she could drink then, at her request, poured the balance over her to help cool her down. All the while she pulled up then reeled, pulled up then reeled.

The midday sun made its presence known some forty-five minutes later. Now there was no shade, no place to hide as the sun perched directly overhead shining brightly and giving off its tropical warmth,

"It's Hot!" Eva exclaimed. Every time she thought she was making progress; her adversary would make a run. The battle between her, the fish and the heat, left her uncertain if she could win this fight. But that was a thought she kept to herself. She knew whatever was hooked would not only ensure her female angler award but it could mean a tournament win. So, she continued to reel. Even though Calhoun had done his best to keep her hydrated, her body was beginning to cramp…everywhere. The clock had moved on toward hour number three when suddenly…it was over.

Eva at first did not recognize what had happened. She was pulling up and reeling down when she realized she did not need to go through that motion anymore. She started to reel straight in, finding a reserve of strength she did not know she had but realizing if she did not boat this fish now, it would indeed get the best of her.

For five solid minutes she reeled while willing her arm not to cramp any further. Bones was leaning over the stern with gaff in hand as well as the billy club if needed when he shouted, "I see it. Oh my God, it's a damn big shark.

"Get ready to club it before you gaff it. I want it dead or at least unconscious before you gaff it." Hank was issuing instructions while studying the fish from the bridge and doing some mental calculations as well.

"Hold up! Calhoun go get the extra rope out of the anchor locker. No way we can bring her on board. She is too big. We will need to lash her to the stern. Mighty fine Blue Shark you just caught Eva. Don't see many around these parts. Congrats!"

Eva slumped in her chair, too exhausted to enjoy the moment.

Chapter Sixty-One

It took about thirty minutes for Hank and Bones to lash the blue shark to the stern. It took about thirty seconds for a crowd to start gathering at Browns Marina for the weigh in once Hank had called it in. With a shark anchored to the stern, the Mahalo was officially done for the tournament as there was no reasonable way to continue fishing with that obstruction situated where it was.

The block and tackle were lowered to the rear of the boat and the fish hoisted up. Weighing in at one hundred eighty-four pounds at a length of just over six feet, it was the largest shark caught during the tournament and established a record for blue sharks caught off Bimini that stood for six years.

However, it presented a problem. There was no category for blue sharks on the leaderboard due to its rarity, so the judges were at a loss as to the number of points it should be allocated. The rarer the fish, the more points it was given for its weight. Currently, a great white was given the most points on a weighted average but the consensus was the blue shark was even more rare so even a higher weighted average per pound should be given to it. In the balance could hang the final results as to the winner of the tournament.

Hank was inclined to stay around and argue his case but Eva would have none of it. "Let the judges decide. I want a shower and a drink, not necessarily in that order and then we can all meander up to the Calypso Club for the awards ceremony and be surprised as to the winner."

"As you say Eva. Your fish, your decision. Anyway, I think we all could use both a drink and a shower." Hank had no sooner spoken those words and backed away from the weigh in station than his heart sank again. Waiting at their slip were now half a dozen police including their friends from the U.S. Marshall's Service.

Chapter Sixty-Two

Once again, with all the dock help it only took moments to secure the Mahalo to her berth. No one on board spoke a word for fear of hearing what they all dreaded…that Slayder somehow had slipped away once again. So, they were stunned when Agent Chewning spoke.

"We have him under surveillance, he has not gone anywhere. We have an informant embedded in his group and the word is he will attempt to leave within the next twenty-four hours. We have the airfield buttoned down and all planes are accounted for with the exception of a DC-3 which is locked up tight and off to the side at one end of the runway."

"Well, the obvious question is why don't you check that plane out…get a warrant or something" snapped Eva.

"It is not that simple since the plane is registered in the states but sits here. Now we are dealing with international laws so our best bet is to grab him once he boards the plane. Therefore, my suggestion is you keep to your schedule, attend the awards banquet tonight and leave tomorrow. By the way, how are you leaving?"

"By plane." Calhoun responded. "My King Air will be here in the morning. Eva and I plan on taking it back to Lauderdale and Hank will wait until he can attach himself to a returning convoy and leave then, which I believe will also be around the time of our departure. Now, I have a question…how does a plane as big as a DC-3 just show up without anyone noticing?"

Captain Shumate took a step forward. "As you may or may not know, this field does not have lights nor is there a control tower. Typically, once a plane leaves Miami airspace, they are handed off to Nassau to monitor since they have no direct sightlines on these out islands. Every pilot usually flies over the airstrip to eyeball whether any plane is getting ready to take off and to also take a look at wind direction by looking at the airsock and the direction it is flying. They squawk on the channel assigned to this field the intention of landing and then just pray everyone else is paying attention and following a similar protocol. The DC-3 came in a couple of nights ago, well after dark and someone used smudge pots to line and light the runway. They land, douse the pots and take them with them and then boat over to Alice Town where they blend in until time to go which we now know will be tomorrow when everyone else is leaving. We will keep the airfield and you guys under surveillance. Yours will be more obvious as several uniformed men will be present with you until such time as you depart for home. The field is under a more covert overwatch. We can watch it without being discovered. So, again, our plan is to catch Slayder as he boards and then he will be arrested and charged."

"Well, I hope your plan works Captain Shumate and Agent Chewning. Now, we have a function to attend so if you don't have anything else, you will excuse us." And with that, Eva effectively slammed the door on any further discussion.

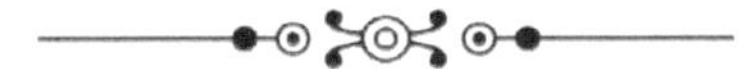

Chapter Sixty-Three

Hank, Calhoun and Eva left at six, the Mahalo in the capable hands of two uniformed policemen, to begin the walk toward the Calypso Club. At the end of the dock Bones waited in the company of an additional three policemen. As they started up the road, one uniform walked slightly ahead of the group with the other two trailing slightly behind. As has become their habit, Bones and Hank flanked Calhoun and Eva who were walking arm in arm. The entourage basically took up the width of the street but no one seemed to mind stepping to the side. Everyone knew of Eva and as they walked, a smattering of applause could be heard amongst a few "Good luck Miss Eva," or "God Bless you, Miss Eva." The spontaneous reception brought tears to Eva's eyes but broadened the smile and swelled the chest of Calhoun with pride for his girlfriend. The EVA project had made her a much-appreciated minor celebrity on the island.

Fifteen minutes later they entered the Calypso Club. Given the fact there were over fifty boats in the tournament along with assorted anglers and crew, the main hall was teeming; mostly with men. The uniformed policemen stepped away from their charges and tried their best just to blend in all the while keeping a sharp eye on the Mahalo crew and observing everyone else. Even though the bar was packed, those patrons also melted away in deference to Eva. She smiled and thought how quickly things could change.

At six-fifteen the tournament chair gaveled the session into order by asking everyone to please find their table. As it happened, the Mahalo was seated alongside the crew from the Tedi Bare. LaRue was in fine spirits, just short of bursting into song. Eva, for one, was glad he did not have his constant companion, Louise, with him.

In order to move the evening along, dinner was served to the various tables allowing the program to go forward at the same time.

"First of all, let me welcome you all and congratulate you on a tightly fought tournament." Announced the Tournament Chairman, George Andrews. He went on to explain how many boats participated and the number of people it brought to the island's economy. After some minor awards and recognitions, it finally came time to announce the three major trophies. "First of all. For top female angler" there followed a long pause in the hopes to build anticipation, "For the second consecutive year...Eva Knox of the Mahalo!" The room rose as one with applause, whistles and catcalls as Eva moved toward the podium to accept her hardware and winner's check. She gladly took it from George, turned and mouthed a thank you to the crowd and returned to her seat.

"For the top male angler, fishing from the Gypsea, Ray Jones!" There was no standing ovation, just polite applause as he went forward to accept his trophy and check. But rather than return to his seat, George asked him to stay up on the podium.

"Ladies and Gentlemen, placing third, Tedi-Bare!" LaRue pushed back his chair and moved forward to accept his winnings.

"Now, for first place. For the first time in the history of this tournament we have a tie!" This news was met with a few gasps and a few playful boos. "The winners of this year's tournament are the Gypsea and…. the Mahalo!" Jeers turned to cheers once the Mahalo was named. Never had a boat leapt over three other boats to win. George raised his hands, palms out, in an effort to get the crowd to quiet down.

"Now the tournament rules allow for only one winner. Gypsea and Mahalo were dead even on points so we had to go to our tie breaker which is the number of fish caught. In this case, Gypsea outpaced the Mahalo by four more boated fish, so the Gypsea is declared the overall winner!"

More boos ensued; these were a bit more vigorous. As Ray walked over to accept his check, he, too, held up his hands for quiet. Once the crowd settled down, he addressed the group.

"I am like you. I feel there should be two winners tonight as we saw an amazing display of sportsmanship from the Mahalo and especially from Eva. As many of you know, Eva has poured her heart into a rescue effort for all the strays on the island often on a shoestring budget. I would like all of you to assist her with her every vessel assists program and donate before you leave here tonight. I, for one, am pleased to announce that this evening's winner's check will be donated to her program to help them continue their rescue efforts".

The roar of approval that instantly followed this announcement was deafening. Eva, with tears in her eyes for the second time this evening, raced to the podium to give Ray a hug as he handed her the endorsed check. The moment was emotional for everyone in the room as the cheers and applause continued seemingly without end. On this evening, there were no losers.

Chapter Sixty-Four

It took them almost a full hour to extricate themselves from the overwhelming rounds of congratulations they were receiving. While some of the older captains directed their attention toward Hank, most of the crowd wanted to say something to Eva and to give her whatever paper money they may have on them for her animal shelter. She collected not only Bahamian cash but U.S. dollars as well as a few checks. In a twist of irony, someone had located a couple of her coconut inspired bowls and used them to hold the collections.

Finally, the crowd thinned out enough allowing the crew of the Mahalo to escape along with their police escort. As before, the police took up the same loose formation they had used on the way to the club.

"Some night!" exclaimed Hank. "Now you have a bunch of cash to count before you leave tomorrow."

"Yep!" a jubilant Eva exclaimed. "I'm too excited to sleep right now anyway so let's count what we have, plan on taking it to the bank first thing in the morning then, Hank, you can drop us on South Bimini and be on your way since it sounds like there are plenty of boats convoying back stateside tomorrow."

"Counting money, sipping on a late-night rum and coke after winning a major tournament sounds like heaven to me," responded the captain as they made the turn to the dock where the Mahalo sat silently waiting.

By the time they had finished counting the money, they had slightly more than eleven thousand dollars plus the winning checks from Ray Jones. More than enough to build a first-rate shelter on the island. Eva's heart was full as she turned in for the evening. Four uniformed policemen surrounded the Mahalo and kept watch during the balance of the night. No one bothered the exhausted inhabitants on this evening.

Chapter Sixty-Five

The routine of getting up early to prepare for a day of fishing found the entire crew in the salon before six, the latest arrival being Eva. "Couldn't sleep." She confessed.

"It's our body clocks." responded Calhoun. "We will get back to a normal sleep pattern in a day or two. Let me just take a moment to tell you all how proud I am of each of you. We came to win and we did. We came to trap Slayder and we did. It is not up to us to capture him too."

Before he could continue, the salon doors opened and Bones popped his head in. "Hope I'm not interrupting" as he plopped his day bag on the couch. "Thought I would ride shotgun with Hank to make sure he gets back okay and I can catch a Chalks flight back tomorrow."

"I appreciate that" Hank said. "You didn't interrupt, the boss was just sharing how he was going to give us all a raise!" he teased.

"As a matter of fact, that was exactly what I was going to do. You may not know there is a reward for Slayder but if we can assist in his capture the reward belongs to us. At least according to Agent Chewning. So, let's stay aware over the next couple of hours. We have a large amount of cash to take to The Bank of the Bahamas branch just down the street and then Al in our King Air should be here around ten this morning to take Eva and I back to Lauderdale."

"You got a new pilot?" quizzed Hank.

"Yep" answered Calhoun. "Al Chaplin. A young guy, played tennis at Kansas State which I like since it indicates he has good reflexes. You need those sometimes when flying. You will meet him shortly. Frank is still with us but he has let us know he is eyeing retirement."

"Well, I'm going below to shower and pack. Let's be at the bank when they open so we can get this money deposited and get on our way. Calhoun, you need to finish packing as well so come on with me" ordered Eva.

As often happened when both Calhoun and Eva disappeared below, it took them quite some time before they reemerged. There would be no such tomfoolery on this day.

Eva and everyone else gathered around the table that morning began a day they would never forget.

Chapter Sixty-Six

Two weeks earlier, as part of a nationwide airport upgrade program, a PAPI (Precision Approach Path Indicator) box was installed at either end of the runway. Standing at six feet tall, it should have been located about twenty feet off the runway allowing pilots to visually confirm they were aligned correctly for their approach. This device was the first of two major upgrades for island landing strips throughout the country. The second was to add lights. Nothing was operational yet so no one had checked to see if the installment was correct. Had they checked, they would have found the box was inside ten feet to the runway creating a clear and potentially fatal aviation hazard.

There had been no problem getting the deposit to the bank and made. How could there be with four uniformed police trailing around every step Eva took?

Packed and ready to go, Eva and Calhoun said their good-byes to two of the uniformed police. The other two would stay with them until they were aboard their plane and the plane had actually taken off. These were the orders of Captain Shumate.

Departing The Big Game Club was bitter sweet for Eva. Her name would soon go up on a plaque, recognizing her as the winning female angler. No one had consecutively repeated that feat until her. The Gypsea and the Mahalo would be named co-winners, this coming at the insistence of Ray Jones, another generous gesture by this world class angler. As of now, no one knew when they may return as no plans had yet to be made.

Shoving off, Calhoun and Eva settled into their respective fighting chairs while the two policemen on escort duty sat on the fish box to face them. Eva quizzed them about their families and all things relative to living on Bimini. Bones was on the flying bridge with Hank for the quick fifteen-minute transit to South Bimini and the airstrip.

As they neared the communal dock restricted for airport use, Hank leaned over the rail. "Mr. Hipp, you better come take a look at this."

Puzzled, Calhoun ascended the ladder to the bridge and was stunned by the sight before him. Lined up along the strip, the grass and any place else they could find were a dozen planes, all of which had their engines warming and all of them jockeying for takeoff position. He immediately spotted the largest of these aircraft, the DC-3 which had to be the plane law enforcement had been keeping watch over.

"My God, it looks like La Guardia at rush hour, only in miniature! And how in the hell did that DC-3 get loose?"

"No way to know since this is an uncontrolled field," responded Hank. "I'm not sure how they are going to sort this out. Obviously, all the planes that brought over kites elected to stay to pick up their charges now they are all trying to leave at once."

About that time a King Air buzzed the field. "That would be Al, doing a clearing turn to make sure the runway is clear before he lands. I'm sure he is squawking on whatever frequency they are on that he's trying to land while everyone else is trying to depart." observed Calhoun.

By now they had reached the dock and with the assistance of their escorts got the Mahalo tied off. The entire crew started to make its way toward the one room customs shack to finalize the paperwork necessary to leave. Outside of it stood a solitary customs agent, clearly flabbergasted by the confusion swirling around the airstrip.

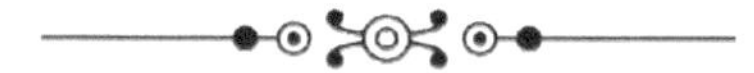

Chapter Sixty-Seven

The first thing Eva noticed above the din of so many airplanes so close together all with their engines running were the ripples in the air. She could actually see the disruption of the air made by a couple of dozen engines disrupting it. It was an otherworldly sight, one which she was ready to get away from especially as she saw the huge DC-3 rumbling toward them using the grassy area to get around those planes which had lined up for takeoff.

At the same time the DC-3 was making its move, Al was buzzing the field for a second time, trying to figure out what was going on, all the while squawking his intention to begin a final approach. Other pilots heard him and acknowledged but it was not those guys he was concerned about. It was the 3, looking like she was going to attempt to take off even with a shortened runway due to the number of planes clustered at one end.

"This is November One Romeo Three Charlie Hotel on final approach Bimini. All aircraft please be advised."

Al did not care about the other aircraft as they were complying, it was the 3 he was worried about.

In the cockpit of the World War Two workhorse, now loaded with marijuana beyond load limits, Slayder turned to his pilot. "Don't sweat this, we got it. If we can sneak aboard while everyone else was heading toward their planes, we can certainly get the cowboy flying that King Air to back down. Let's go!"

The pilot gave Slayder a look that was a combination of doubt and fear but he knew better than to argue. He stood on his breaks, revved the engines to maximum torque released the brakes and started his roll just as several policemen emerged from the underbrush, one even so brazen as to take a shot at one of the tires, grazing it but causing a slow leak which got worse the further the plane hobbled down the runway. She was grabbing for all the lift she could find. The pilots' eyes were so fixed on his instruments that he did not see the PAPI building until Slayder yelled "LOOK OUT!".

Too late, the plane was simply too heavy and had not achieved enough lift to avoid the structure, the right wing clipping it. As if in slow motion the DC-3 tried to claw her way into the air but the law of physics took over as she began to pinwheel before the pilot lost all control and the old war horse pancaked into the ocean about fifty yards from shore where she quickly sunk.

Hank, along with several of the policemen were at a dead run to get to the plane. In the meantime, Al had pulled out of his landing approach and now did circles over the crash site in the hopes of spotting someone emerging from the wreckage.

Two of the policemen were first on the scene and after making several dives on the plane, gave up and came ashore. "No survivors" came the terse report. "We can see thru the windscreen. Both pilots are still strapped in and it appears they both may have broken their necks on impact."

Eva gasped at the news, shuddering into Calhoun's arms. In the meantime, the air overhead was disrupted by the landing Al was attempting. All the other planes shut down their engines. Those pilots were now witnesses to a plane crash which involved loss of life. They knew they would be here awhile filling out reports and answering questions from police even though there were almost as many police who had witnessed the crash as pilots.

Chapter Sixty-Eight

With so many witnesses, particularly so many in law enforcement, it did not take long to get and verify everyone's statement as to what had occurred. By four that afternoon almost all were released, the most notable asked to stay over was Al as Captain Shumate just wanted to make sure none of his actions forced the DC-3 down.

"Well," observed Calhoun, "looks like the best way back is by boat. There are several leaving now that the show is over."

Before he could continue, Eva interjected. "Let's go and let's go now." She had been traumatized by the sudden and rapid demise of her former adversary. She wanted to get away and do so immediately. Bones elected to stay behind now that Calhoun and Eva were on board with Hank. He said his good-byes with a heavy heart. He knew it would take some time for Eva to get past what had occurred this morning and he knew he would most likely not see her until she was ready to face those demons.

That evening, divers brought up the two bodies from the cockpit, one was positively identified as Slayder, the other had no identification on him making the task of discovering who he was a little more challenging. The bales of marijuana were off loaded the next day to be disposed of by the local authorities. For years later, the DC-3 sat where it had crashed, in a watery grave for all to see through the crystal green waters of the shallows off of South Bimini. It became a favorite snorkeling site for tourists and gathering spot for local lobsters.

Chapter Sixty-Nine

They sat in their respective fighting chairs as Hank guided the Mahalo home. Both were lost in thought so Calhoun was surprised when Eva reached over grabbed and held his hand. "I just want to feel alive again." Hank had moved to the rail surrounding the bridge and could not help overhearing her. "I tell you what Eva, if you will look left for the next minute or so, I think you might be buoyed by what you see. Keep your eyes on the sunset, especially the trailing edge just before it sinks below the horizon.

She did as instructed and less than five minutes later was rewarded by a green flash coming from the sunset as it sank below the horizon. It barely lasted the length of a wink but there it was and Hank had proved correct…it lifted her spirits immensely.

"I have always heard about that flash but had never seen one. Thanks Captain!"

"My pleasure" he said as he moved back to the captain's chair. He felt good about the week, all in all. Now it was time to get home to his family.

Calhoun looked over and gave a squeeze to Eva's hand. "You okay?" She nodded that she was. He swung his arm in a wide arc saying, "All of this reminds me of one of the quotes from Dante's book you have been reading

She gave him a quizzical look as he continued. "'Remember tonight for it is the beginning of always.'"

She smiled and looked deep into his eyes. Her heart was content as she knew his was as well.

"Calhoun?"

"Mmmm?"

"I'm pregnant."

Epilogue

Three months later and some four hundred miles away, two men walked thru an outer gate comprised of a thirty-foot-tall barbed wire topped chain link fence. Tom and Jerry, better known as the Cartoon Gang so derisively named by Calhoun the very first time he met Eva, were finally free and with one thought on their minds…. Revenge.

Appendix A

As I explained in my first book, Hank had to be a master of many trades, not the least of which was chef. I know I ate a great deal of his cooking and it was always extraordinary. I included one of his recipes in Mahalo Memories and continue that tradition here.

Hank's Black Beans
4 cans black beans
8 strips bacon – chopped
Onion – chopped
½ each red, yellow and green peppers
Maple syrup – a squirt
Garlic
Hot Sauce – 1 shot
Soy Sauce – Good shot (his words not mine)
Black Pepper

Fry bacon until brown in pan. Add onions, peppers and garlic. In large pot put beans,

syrup, hot sauce, pepper. Add bacon and bacon
grease from fry pan. Simmer ½ hour or so.
Serve with a shot of Sherry

And finally, go mix a rum and coke with a lime
and give a toast to the crew of The Mahalo!

About the Author

Boyd Hipp is currently a full time commercial real estate broker whenever he is not writing. A former real estate developer with communities in the two Carolinas, Georgia and Florida he now spends his time in upstate South Carolina not far from his five children and especially not far from his ten grandchildren.

He is a graduate of Wofford College (BA) and the University of South Carolina (MBA).

www.ingramcontent.com/pod-product-compliance
Lightning Source LLC
Chambersburg PA
CBHW022132050726
47590CB00002B/512